## "Does the cal[...]
## ever get exha[...]

Zach didn't care for how easily Daisy saw through him. "Who says it's a facade?"

Her mouth quirked up at one side. "You weren't so bland or bored when I was rifling through your stuff."

Even now the reminder made his jaw clench, even more so when she full-on grinned and pointed at him. "See? Underneath that robot exterior, there is a man with a living, breathing heart." She looked down at the guitar in her lap and frowned. "Believe it or not, Zach, I'd rather have a man with a heart on this case over a robot."

"Believe it or not, Daisy, I do what I have to do to keep you safe. Robot exterior included."

She pursed her lips together, as if she took it as some kind of challenge.

Lucky for him, he was not a man to back down from a challenge—any more than he was a man to lose one.

# WYOMING COWBOY BODYGUARD

## Nicole Helm

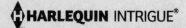

For the female songwriters in country music whose songs make up the bulk of my book soundtracks, thank you for the inspiration.

ISBN-13: 978-1-335-64095-6

Wyoming Cowboy Bodyguard

Copyright © 2019 by Nicole Helm

Recycling programs for this product may not exist in your area.

Printed in U.S.A.

www.Harlequin.com

**Nicole Helm** grew up with her nose in a book and the dream of one day becoming a writer. Luckily, after a few failed career choices, she gets to follow that dream—writing down-to-earth contemporary romance and romantic suspense. From farmers to cowboys, Midwest to *the* West, Nicole writes stories about people finding themselves and finding love in the process. She lives in Missouri with her husband and two sons and dreams of someday owning a barn.

## Books by Nicole Helm

### Harlequin Intrigue

#### Carsons & Delaneys: Battle Tested

*Wyoming Cowboy Marine*
*Wyoming Cowboy Sniper*
*Wyoming Cowboy Ranger*
*Wyoming Cowboy Bodyguard*

#### Carsons & Delaneys

*Wyoming Cowboy Justice*
*Wyoming Cowboy Protection*
*Wyoming Christmas Ransom*

*Stone Cold Texas Ranger*
*Stone Cold Undercover Agent*
*Stone Cold Christmas Ranger*

### Harlequin Superromance

#### A Farmers' Market Story

*All I Have*
*All I Am*
*All I Want*

*Falling for the New Guy*
*Too Friendly to Date*
*Too Close to Resist*

Visit the Author Profile page at Harlequin.com.

# CAST OF CHARACTERS

*Zach Simmons*—Former FBI agent, currently partnered with Cam Delaney in a security company called CD Corp that offers protection for those in danger. Zach's brainchild is a ghost town used as cover for a thriving protective community.

*Daisy Delaney/Lucy Cooper*—Famous country singer Daisy Delaney's real name is Lucy Cooper, and she's been stalked for the past year, culminating in her bodyguard's murder. Worried that her brother's family will be in danger if she stays in Texas, she agrees to go to Wyoming to be protected by CD Corp.

*Vaughn Cooper*—Lucy's brother, a Texas Ranger who arranges all her security after her bodyguard's death.

*Cam Delaney*—Zach's business partner in CD Corp, also engaged to Zach's sister. They take turns being lead on cases, so he's only doing research on Daisy's case.

*Hilly Adams*—Zach's sister, who grew up apart from the family. She's the assistant at CD Corp and helps with running errands.

*Jordan Jones*—Daisy's ex-husband, also a famous country singer. He's been attempting to make Daisy look bad in the press since their divorce, which she instigated.

*Stacy Vine*—Daisy's manager and friend since she was a teenager.

# Chapter One

Tom was dead. She'd been ushered away from his lifeless body and open, empty brown eyes thirty minutes ago and still, that was all she saw. Tom sprawled on the floor, limbs at an unnatural angle, eyes open and unseeing.

Blood.

She was in the back of a police cruiser, moving through Austin at a steady clip. Daisy Delaney. America's favorite country bad girl. Until she'd filed for divorce from country's golden child, Jordan Jones. Now everyone hated her, and someone wanted her dead.

But they'd killed Tom first.

She wanted to close her eyes, but she was afraid the vision of Tom would only intensify if she did. So she focused on the world out the window. Pearly dawn. Green suburban lawns.

She was holding it together. Even though Tom's lifeless eyes haunted her. And all that blood. The smell of it. She was queasy and desperately wanted to cry, but she was holding on. *Gotta save face, Daisy girl. No matter what. Never let them see they got to you.*

It didn't matter the name her mother had given her was Lucy Cooper. Daddy had always used her stage name—the name *he'd* given her. Daisy Delaney, after his dearly departed grandmother, who'd given him his first guitar.

She'd relished that once upon a time, no matter how much her mother and brother had disapproved. Today, for the first time in her life, she wondered where she might be if she hadn't followed in her famous father's footsteps.

She couldn't change the past so she held it together. Didn't let anyone see she was devastated, shaken or scared.

Until the car pulled up in front of her brother's house. He was standing outside. She'd expected to see him in his Texas Rangers uniform of pressed khakis, a button-up shirt and that shiny star she knew he took such pride in.

Instead, he was in sweats, a baby cradled in his arms.

"You shouldn't have brought me here," she whispered to the police officer as he shifted into Park.

"Ranger Cooper asked me to, ma'am."

She let out a breath. Asked. While her brother was a Texas Ranger and this man was Austin PD, Daisy was under no illusions her brother hadn't interfered enough to make sure it was an order, not a request.

When the officer opened the door for her, she managed a smile and a thank-you. The officer shook hands with Vaughn, then gave her a sympathetic look. "We'll have more questions for you, Ms. Delaney, but the ones you answered at the scene will do for now."

She smiled thinly. "Thank you. And if there's any break in the case—"

"We'll let you and your brother know."

The officer nodded and left. Daisy turned to Vaughn.

"You shouldn't have brought me here," she said, peeking into the bundle of blankets. She brushed her fingers over her niece's cheek. "It isn't safe having me around you guys."

"Safety's my middle name," Vaughn said, and there wasn't an ounce of concern or fear in his voice, but she could feel it nonetheless. Her straitlaced brother had never understood her need to follow their father's spotlight, but he'd always been her protector. "You didn't tell me you'd come back to Austin."

She'd thought she could keep it from him.

Keep him and Nat from worrying when they had this gorgeous little family they were building.

Daisy had been stupid and foolish to think she'd be able to keep anything from Vaughn. She couldn't afford to be stupid and foolish anymore. Though she'd lived in fear for almost a year now, she'd believed it would remain a nonviolent threat. Her stalker had never hurt her or anyone she'd been connected to.

Now he'd killed Tom. The man Vaughn had hired to protect her. It wasn't her own failure. Rationally, she knew that, but kind, funny Tom, who'd done everything in his power to protect her, was dead.

"Come inside, Lucy." Vaughn slid his free arm around her shoulders and the first tear fell over onto her cheek. She couldn't let more fall, and yet her brother's steadiness, and the name only he and Mom called her, was one of the few things that could undo her.

Well, that and murder, she supposed. "Tom…"

"We'll handle the arrangements," Vaughn said, squeezing her shoulders as baby Nora gurgled happily in her daddy's arms. "He was a good man."

"He shouldn't have died protecting me."

"But he did. He signed up for that job. You'll have time to mourn that. We all will, but right now we need to focus on getting you somewhere safe."

She wanted to say something snotty. Vaughn could be so cold, and though she knew it was his law-enforcement training, it grated. Except he held his baby like the precious gift she was, and Daisy had watched years ago as his voice had broken when he'd made his vows to his wife.

Vaughn wasn't cold or heartless. He just had control down to an art form. And his concern was her. Daisy felt like such a burden to him, and yet there was no way to convince him this wasn't his problem.

"Nat's got coffee on and Jaime is on his way over," Vaughn said, locking the door behind her then leading her up the stairs of his split-level ranch.

"What's Jaime got to do with this?" Daisy asked warily. "You can't get the FBI involved. I—"

"I'm not getting the FBI involved. I'm using my FBI connections to find a safe place for you while we let the professionals investigate."

"And by professionals you mean you."

"I mean anyone and everyone I can get on this case. With our connection, I'm not legally allowed to be part of the official investigation."

Which meant he'd launch his own unofficial

one. No matter how by-the-book Vaughn was, he'd always break rules for his loved ones.

Nat came out of the kitchen as they crested the stairs. She pulled Daisy into a hard hug. "How are you?" she asked, brown eyes full of compassion.

Daisy had no questions about how Vaughn had fallen for Natalie, but she did have some questions about the reverse.

"Unscathed."

Natalie pursed her lips. "Physically. Which wasn't all I meant." She eyed her husband. "Coopers," she muttered with some disgust, though Daisy knew—for as little time as she managed to spend with her family here due to her crazy touring schedule—Nat spoke with love.

The doorbell rang, Nora fussed and Nat and Vaughn exchanged the baby and words with the choreographed practice of marriage. It caused a multitude of pangs in Daisy.

Her divorce had started the press's character assassination—thanks to Jordan's team, who were desperate to keep his star on the rise.

Then the stalking had started, and everything had become a numb kind of blank.

But she could still remember marrying Jordan with the hope she'd have something like Nat and Vaughn had. That had been a joke.

"Sit down. You want to hold Nora for me? I've got to go check on Miranda." Nat was maneuvering her onto the couch, placing tiny Nora into her arms and hurrying off to check on their other daughter as Vaughn and his brother-in-law ascended the stairs.

"Ah, the cavalry," Daisy said with a wry twist of her lips.

"Good to see you again, Daisy," Jaime Alessandro greeted. An FBI agent, married to Natalie's sister, Daisy had met him on a few occasions. He was more personable than Vaughn, but the whole FBI thing made Daisy uneasy.

"Let's get straight to it, then," Vaughn said, taking a seat next to Daisy on the couch. Jaime settled himself on an armchair across from them.

"I'm sure you know how concerned Vaughn's been even before the murder."

Daisy eyed her brother. "No. You don't say."

Jaime smiled. Vaughn didn't.

"We've been looking into some options, along with the investigation. As long as the stalker continues to evade police, the prime goal is keeping you safe. To that end, I have an idea."

"That sounds ominous coming from an FBI agent."

"How do you feel about Wyoming?"

"Cold," Daisy replied dryly.

"I have a friend I was in Quantico with. He has a security business. I talked to him about your situation and he came up with a plan. It involves isolating you."

"I was isolated before. The cabin—"

"Is isolated, but not completely off the grid," Vaughn said of their old family cabin that had been vandalized during her last hiding stint. "It was traceable, and you've been easy to follow. We're going to take extra precautions to make sure you aren't followed to Wyoming."

Daisy wanted to close her eyes, but she shifted Nora in her arms and looked down at the baby instead. "So you want me to secretly jet off to Wyoming and then what?"

"And then you're safe while we find this guy. This is murder now. Things are escalating, which means everyone else's investigation is going to escalate."

"We can have you there by tomorrow afternoon," Jaime said. "They'll be ready for you."

Part of her wanted to argue, but Tom's lifeless body flashed into her mind. She didn't want to die. Not like that. And more, so much more, she didn't want Vaughn or his precious family in the crosshairs.

"Just tell me what I need to do."

ZACH SIMMONS SURVEYED the town. It looked like every picture of a ghost town he'd ever seen. Empty, windowless buildings. Dusty dirt road that would have once been a bustling Main Street. You could feel the history, and the utter emptiness.

It was perfect.

He grinned over at his soon-to-be brother-in-law and business partner. "Still worried about the investment?"

Cam Delaney eyed him. "Hell yes, I'm still worried." He scanned the dilapidated buildings and the way the mountains jutted out in the distance, like sentries, in Zach's mind. This would be a place of protection. Of safety.

"This job's a big one for your first."

Zach nodded. He was under no illusions this wasn't a giant challenge. Tricky and messy and complicated. He couldn't explain to Cam, or anyone really, how thrilling it was to be out of the confines of the FBI's rules and regulations. He wouldn't take his time back as an agent for anything, but it had been stifling in the end.

So stifling he'd ended up getting himself kicked out.

This was better. Even if the first job was with some spoiled country singer star who'd gotten herself in a mess of trouble. Probably her own doing. But she was in trouble, and Zach and Cam's security company was getting paid, seriously paid, to keep her safe.

"Laurel come up with any connection to you guys?" Zach asked, hoping Daisy Delaney's last name was a coincidence. Not that he'd tell anyone, but all the Carson and Delaney coupling worried him a little.

He was technically a Carson, though his mother had run away from her family at eighteen and only started reconnecting this year. He told himself he didn't believe in curses or the Carson-Delaney feud the town of Bent, Wyoming, was so invested in.

So invested, Main Street was practically split down the middle—Carson businesses on one side, Delaney businesses on the other. Then there was the curse talk, which said if a Carson and Delaney were ever friendly, or God forbid, romantic, only bad things would befall Bent.

But over the course of the past year Carsons and Delaneys had been falling for each other left and right, and while there'd been a certain uptick in trouble in Bent, everything and everyone was fine.

Which his cousins and their significant others had turned into believing it was all meant to be, and went on and on about love solving things.

Zach didn't buy an inch of either belief— but still, the idea of a Delaney under his protection gave him a bit of a worried itch.

"She's still researching. It's giving her something to do now that she's on maternity leave. Baby should come any day, though, so I'm not sure she'll come up with any answers one way or another. You can always ask the woman."

Zach shrugged. "Doesn't matter either way."

Cam chuckled. "Sure. You're not worried about what might happen if she's some long-lost cousin of mine?"

"No, I'm not. I'm worried about keeping Daisy Delaney safe from her stalker, assuming there really is one." Because the Daisy Delaney case would set the tone for what he wanted to offer here. On the surface it would look like a ghost town. But below the surface it could be a place for people to find safety, security and hope while the slow wheels of justice handled things legally.

If he believed in life callings, and these days he was starting to, his was this. He'd been a part of the slow wheels of justice. He'd failed at protecting because of it. Now he'd do all he could to keep those entrusted to him safe.

"I should head off to the airport. You'll do the double check?"

Cam nodded. "Is turndown service offered as part of the package?"

"Up to you, boss," Zach said with a grin, slapping Cam on the back.

Cam eyed him, but Zach ignored the perceptive look and headed for his car. He didn't need Cam giving him another lecture about taking things slow, having reasonable expectations for a fledgling business.

Zach had endured a bad year. Really bad. His brother had been admitted to a psychiatric ward, and his long-lost sister had forgiven the man who'd murdered their father and kidnapped her. He'd been kicked out of the FBI—which meant no hope of ever getting back into legitimate law enforcement. And then he'd tried to help one of his cousins outwit a stalker-murderer and been hurt in the process.

In some ways all that hardship had brought him everything he'd ever wanted—his long-lost sister back in his life, a job that didn't seem to choke the very life out of him and some closure over the murder of his father.

Then there was this project. Ghost Town. He couldn't tamp down his enthusiasm, his excitement. He had to grab on to the rightness he finally felt and hold on to it with everything he had.

He didn't want to go back. He wanted to move forward.

Daisy Delaney was going to be the way to do that. He drove down deserted Wyoming roads to the highway, then to the regional airport in Dubois where his first client would be landing any minute.

Zach parked and entered the small airport, all the excitement of a new job still buzzing inside him.

He'd facilitated crisscrossing flights with his former FBI buddy, and only Zach knew the disguise she'd be wearing. Though he wondered how much a wig and sunglasses would do for a famous singer.

Zach liked country music as much as the next guy, so it was impossible not to know Daisy Delaney's music. She'd somehow eclipsed even her father's outlaw country reputation with wild songs about drinking, cheating and revenge. Country fans either loved her or loved to complain about her.

Of course, since her divorce from all-American sweetheart Jordan Jones, the complainers had gotten more vocal. Zach hadn't followed it all, but he'd read up on it once this assignment had come along. She'd been eviscerated in the press, even when the stalking started. Many thought it was a publicity ploy to get people to feel sorry for her.

It had *not* worked.

Zach couldn't deny it was a possibility, even if a man was dead—the security guard. A shame. But that didn't mean it wasn't a ploy. You never knew with the rich and famous.

Still, Zach was determined to make his own conclusions about Daisy Delaney and what might be going on with her stalker, or fictional stalker as the case may be.

The small crowd walked through the security gates. He'd been told to look for black hair and clothes, a red bag and purple cowboy boots. He spotted her immediately.

In person, she was surprisingly petite. She didn't exactly look like a woman who'd burn your house down if you looked at another woman the wrong way, but looks could be deceiving.

He'd done enough undercover work to know that well.

He adjusted his hat, gave the signal he'd told her people to expect and she nodded and walked over to him.

"You must be Mr. Hughes." She used the fake name Jaime had chosen and held out a hand. The sunglasses she wore hid her eyes, and the mass of black hair hid most of her face. Whatever her emotions were, they were well hidden. Which was good. It wouldn't do to have nerves radiating off her.

He took her outstretched hand and shook it. "And you must be Ms. Bravo." Fake names, but soon enough they wouldn't need to bother with that. "Any more bags?" he asked, nodding to the lone duffel bag she carried.

She shook her head.

"Follow me."

She eyed everyone in the airport as they walked outside, but her shoulders and stride were relaxed as she kept up with him. She didn't fidget or dart. If she was fearing her life, she knew how to hide it.

He opened the passenger-side door to his car. She slid inside. Still no sign of concern over getting into a car with a stranger. Zach frowned as he skirted the car to the driver's side.

But he wiped the frown into a placid expression as he slid into his seat. "We have about a thirty-minute drive ahead of us." He pushed the car into Drive and pulled out of the airport parking lot. "You could take your wig off," he offered. "Get comfortable."

"I'd prefer to wait."

He nodded as he drove. Tough case. A

hint of nerves here and there, but overall a very cool customer. Cautious, though, so she clearly took the threat of danger seriously.

He drove in silence through the middle of nowhere Wyoming. He flicked a few glances her way, though it was hard to discern anything. He didn't get the impression she was impressed, but he hadn't expected her to be. He imagined she preferred, if not the glitz and glam of the city, the slow ease of wealthy Southern life she was probably used to.

Wyoming wouldn't offer that, but it would offer her security. He drove down the main street that was now his domain, this ghost town he and Cam had bought outright.

At some point they'd all be safe houses. Or maybe even a functioning town behind the facade of desertion and decay.

For right now, though, it was just the main house. He pulled up in front of the giant showpiece.

It had been built over a century ago by some railroad executive. From the outside the windows were all knocked out, the wood was faded and peeling paint hung off. Everything sagged, and it had the faint air of haunted house.

It made him grin every time. "Well, here we are."

For the first time he could read her expression. Pure, unadulterated horror. He'd be lying if he said he didn't get a little kick out of that. "I promise it's not as bad as it looks."

She wrenched her gaze away from the large house, then stared at him through the dark sunglasses. "Can I see your ID or something?" she demanded.

He shifted and pulled his wallet out of his pocket and handed it to her. "Have at it." He pushed open the door and got out of the car. "When you're ready, I'll show you where you'll be staying."

## Chapter Two

What Daisy really wanted to do was call her brother and ask him if he'd lost his mind. Call Jaime and ask if she was sure this guy was sane. Call anyone to take her home.

But inside the wallet the man had so casually handed her was a driver's license with the name Jaime had given her. The picture matched the man currently standing in front of the horror-movie house outside the car. There were also all sorts of security licenses and weapon certifications.

Vaughn had said this place was isolated, even more isolated than their old family cabin in the Guadalupe Mountains. But she hadn't been able to picture how that was possible.

*Oh*, was it possible. Possible and horrifying.

She flipped the wallet closed and then looked at the giant, falling-apart building. If she didn't die because a stalker was after her, she'd die because this building was going to fall in on her.

It had to be infested with rats. And probably all other manner of vermin.

She couldn't get her body to move from the safety of this car, and still, the man whom she'd been assured would keep her safe stood outside, grinning at the dilapidated building in front of him.

He wasn't sane. He couldn't be. She was stuck in the middle of nowhere Wyoming with an insane person.

But Vaughn would never let that happen. So she forced herself to get out of the car and slung the duffel bag over her shoulder. She tried not to mourn that she hadn't been able to bring her guitar. This wasn't a musical writing escape. It was literally running for her life.

She stepped next to Zach. She still didn't trust him, but she trusted her brother. She looked up at the building like Zach Simmons did, though not with nearly the amount of reverence he had in his expression.

"I know it looks intimidating from the outside, but that's kind of the point."

"The point?" Daisy asked, studying a board that hung haphazardly from a bent nail.

"From the outside, no one would guess anyone's been here for decades."

"Try centuries," she muttered.

He motioned her forward and she followed him up a cracked and sunken rock pathway to the front door.

"Watch the hole," he announced cheerfully, pointing at the gaping hole in the floorboards of the porch. He shoved a key into the front door and pushed open the creaky, uneven entry. "Even if someone started poking around, all they'd see is decay."

*Yes, that is all I see.* She looked around. She had to admit that although everything appeared to be in a state of decay, there were some important things missing. She didn't see any dust or spiderwebs. Debris, sure. Peeling wallpaper and warped floorboards, check, but it didn't smell like she'd expected it to. There was the faint hint of paint on the air.

He led her over the uneven flooring, then pushed a key into another lock. When this door opened she actually gasped.

The room on the other side was beautiful. Clean and furnished, and though there were no windows, somehow the light he switched on bounced off the colors of the walls and filled the room enough that it didn't feel dank and interior.

"This is the common area," Zach said. And maybe he wasn't totally insane. "Then over there past the sitting area is the kitchen. You're free to use it and anything inside as much as you like. Once we ascertain that you weren't followed on any leg of your trip, you'll be able to venture out more freely, but for now you'll have to stay put."

Daisy could only nod dumbly. Was this real? Maybe *she'd* gone insane. A break with reality following a stressful tragedy.

He locked the door behind them, which was enough to jolt Daisy back to the reality of being in a strange ghost town with a man she didn't know.

But he simply moved forward to a set of two doors. "Your bedroom and bathroom are through here." He unlocked the one on the right.

"What's that one?" she asked, pointing to the door on the left as he pushed the unlocked door open.

"That's where I'll stay."

"You'll… Right." He'd be right next door. This stranger. Hired to protect her, and yet she didn't know him. Even Vaughn didn't know him, and Jaime hadn't known him since they'd trained together in the FBI. Why were they all so trusting?

He handed her the key he'd just used to un-lock the door. "This is yours. I don't have a copy. The outside doors are always locked up in multiple places, so how and when you want to lock your room is up to you."

She knew he was trying to set her at ease, but she could only think of a million ways he could get into the room even without a key. Or anyone could.

People could always get to you if they wanted to badly enough.

He studied her for a moment, then gestured her inside. "You can settle in. Make yourself at home however you need to. Rest, if you'd like."

"Is it that obvious?"

"You've been through an ordeal. Take your time to get acquainted with the place. I'm going to do a routine double check to make sure you weren't followed from Austin. If you need me…" He moved over to the wall, motioned her over.

Hesitantly, she stepped closer, still clutching her bag on her shoulder. He tapped a spot on the wallpaper. "See how this flower has a green bloom and a green stem instead of a blue flower like the rest?"

She nodded wearily.

He pushed on the green flower and a little panel popped out of the wall. Inside was a speaker with a button below it. "Simple speaker to speaker. You need something, you can just buzz me through here. I can either answer, or come over, depending."

He closed the panel and it snapped shut, seamless with the wallpaper once again. How on earth had her life become some kind of… spy movie? "You've thought of everything, haven't you?"

He smiled briefly—something like pride and affection lighting up the blank, bland expression. Just a little flash of personality, and for one surprising moment all she could really think was *gee, he's hot.*

"That's what they pay me for." Then the blankness was back and whatever had sparkled in his blue eyes was gone. Everything about him screamed *cop* again, or, she supposed in his case, *FBI.* It was all the same to her. Law and order didn't suit her the way it had her brother, but she'd be grateful for it in the midst of her current situation.

She studied the room around her. Gleaming hardwood with pretty blue rugs here and there. Floral wallpaper and shabby-chic fixtures. The furniture looked antique—old and a little scarred but well polished. The quilt over the bed looked like it belonged in a pretty farmhouse with billowing lace curtains.

It was calming and comforting, and in a

better state of mind she might even be able to ignore all the facades and locks and intercoms and the lack of windows. But she wasn't in the state of mind to forget that Tom, who'd been paid to protect her, was dead.

"Settle in, Ms. Delaney. You're safe here. I promise you that."

She carefully placed her duffel bag on the shiny hardwood floor. Exhaustion made her body feel as heavy as lead, and she went ahead and lowered herself onto the bed with its pretty quilt. "I'm not safe anywhere, Mr. Simmons."

He opened his mouth to argue, but she wasn't in the mood, so she waved him toward the door. "But I feel safe enough to take a nice long nap, if you'll excuse me."

He raised an eyebrow, presumably at her regal tone and the way she waved him off, but she was too tired to care.

He moved to the door, twisted the lock on the interior knob, then closed the door behind him as he exited.

Daisy took off the wig and then let herself fall into sleep.

ZACH SPENT THE afternoon going over the information he'd been given about Daisy's stalking, and the information he'd gathered himself in anticipation of her arrival.

The murder of her bodyguard while she'd been on stage was certainly the tipping point. The formal investigation had been lax up to that point. Except for the private one her brother had launched.

Zach appreciated the detail of Ranger Cooper's intel, and since he knew too well the stress and helplessness of trying to keep a sibling safe, Zach was grateful for his willingness to share.

Still, there were things that had been missed—well, maybe not missed. Overlooked. Probably still not fair. One of the things that had allowed Zach to do so well in the FBI was his ability to work out patterns, to find threads and connect them in ways other people couldn't.

The stellar way he'd handled himself as an agent prior to his brother's involvement in a case and Zach going rogue was what had kept him from having a splashier, more painful termination from the FBI.

He shrugged away the tension in his shoulders. He hated that it still bothered him, because even if he could rewind time, he'd do most things the same.

Daisy's doorknob turned, and she took one

tentative step out. She'd finally ditched the heavy black wig, and her straight blond hair was pulled back into a ponytail. She'd done something to her face—it'd take him a little more time to get to know her face well enough to know exactly what. If he had to guess, though, he'd say she'd freshened her makeup.

She'd changed out of the sleek black outfit into a long baggy shirt the color of a midsummer sky and black leggings. On her feet she wore thick bright purple socks.

She'd been in there for five hours, and from the looks of it, she'd spent most of the time sleeping—unless her makeup magically fixed the pallor of her skin and the dark circles under her eyes.

"Got any food in this joint?"

He stood and walked over to the side of the common area that acted as a kitchen. "Fully stocked kitchen, which of course you're welcome to. Tell me what you want to make and I'll show you where everything is and how to work everything."

"Coffee. Scratch that. Coffee hasn't been settling lately." She sighed, some of that weary exhaustion in her voice even if it didn't show in her face.

"My suggestion? Hot chocolate and a doughnut."

A smile twitched at the corner of her mouth. "That's enough sugar to fell a horse."

He scoffed. "Amateur hour."

She sighed. "It sounds good. I guess if I'm stuck with a crazed psychopath ready to kill those who protect me, I shouldn't worry about a few extra calories."

"I think you'll live."

She rolled her eyes. "You've never read the comments on photos of women online, have you? Still." She waved a hand to encompass the kitchen. "Lead the way."

"You sit. I'll make it. We'll go over where everything is in the kitchen tomorrow. You get a pass today."

"Gee, thanks." But she didn't argue. She sat and poked at his stacks of notes. "That's a lot of paperwork for keeping me out of trouble."

"Investigating things takes some paperwork," he returned, collecting ingredients for hot chocolate.

"I thought you were just supposed to keep me safe while Vaughn and the police figured it all out."

He slid the mug into the microwave hidden in a cabinet and put a doughnut onto a plate. "I could, but that's not what CD Corp is all about."

"CD Corp sounds like the lamest comic villain organization ever."

"It's meant to be bland, boring and inconspicuous." He walked over and set the plate in front of her.

She smiled up at him. "Mission accomplished."

"And this mission," he said, tapping the papers, "is keeping you safe by understanding the threat against you." Not noticing the little dimple that winked in her cheek or the way her blue eyes reminded him of summer. "Anything I can do to profile or find a pattern allows me to better keep you secure."

"Can I help?"

He turned away, back to hot chocolate prep and to shake off that weird and unfortunate bolt of attraction. Still, his voice was easy and bland when he spoke. "I'm counting on it." He stirred the hot chocolate and then set that next to her before taking his seat in front of his computer.

"Have you noticed the pattern of incidents?" he asked, studying her reaction to the question.

With a nap under her belt, she didn't seem as cold and detached as she had on the ride over. But she also didn't seem as ready to break as she had when he'd shown her her room hours ago. As they'd walked through the safe house earlier, he'd finally seen some signs of exhaustion, suspicion and fear.

Now all those things were still evident, but she seemed to have better control over them. He supposed singers, being performers, had to have a little actor in them, as well. She was good at it, but it had frayed at the edges when he'd told her she was safe.

She'd shored up those edges, but there was a wariness and an exhaustion, not sleep related, haunting her eyes.

"The pattern that they always happen when I'm on stage? Yes, my brother pointed that out, but as I pointed out to him, that's just means and opportunity or whatever phrase you guys use. They know exactly where I'll be and for how long."

"Sure, but I'm talking about the connection to your songs."

She frowned, taking a sip of the hot chocolate.

"The incidents, including the murder of your security guard, always crop up in the few weeks after one of your singles drops on the radio. Not all of them, but I compiled a list of titles."

"Let me guess. The drinking, cheating and swearing songs?"

"No. There's not a thematic connection that I can find." Though he'd look, and would keep considering that angle. "But the connection right now seems to be that things escalate when the songs you wrote yourself do well."

She put down the doughnut she'd lifted to her lips without taking a bite. "That doesn't make any sense."

"Not yet. I figure if we pull on it, it will."

"How did you…"

He shrugged. "I'm good with patterns."

"Good with or genius with?"

He smiled at her, couldn't help it. He'd been trained as an undercover FBI agent. Took on whatever role he had to. He'd learned to hide himself underneath a million masks, but his personal attachment to this job and the safe world he'd created made it hard to do here. "Hate to bandy a word like *genius* around."

She laughed and for a brief second her eyes lit with humor instead of worry. He wanted to be able to give that to her permanently, so she could laugh and relax and feel *safe* here.

Because that was his job, his duty, what he was good at. Completely irrelevant to the specific woman he was helping.

He looked down at his computer, frowning

at the uncomfortable and unreasonable pull of emotion inside him. Emotions were what had gotten him booted from the FBI in the first place. He didn't regret it—couldn't—but it was a dangerous line to walk when your emotions got involved.

"So, I think we can rule out crazed fan. It's more personal than that."

"Fans create a personal connection to you, though. They think they know you through your music—whether it was written by me or someone else doesn't matter to them."

"It matters to someone," Zach returned. "Or the incidents wouldn't align so perfectly with the songs you wrote."

She pushed out of her chair, doughnut untouched, only a few sips of the hot chocolate taken. She paced. He waited. When she seemed to accept he wasn't going to say anything, she whirled toward him.

"Look, I don't know how to do this."

"Do what?"

"Hide and cower and…" She gave the chair she'd popped out of a violent shove, then raked shaking hands through her hair. "A good man is dead because of me. I can't stand it."

The naked emotion, brief though it was, hit him a little hard, so he kept his tone brusque. "A good man is dead because good men die in the pursuit of doing good and because there are forces and people out there who aren't so good. Guilt's normal, but you'll need to work it out."

"Oh, will I?"

"I'd recommend therapy, once this is sorted."

"Therapy," she echoed, like he was speaking a foreign language.

"Stalking is basically a personal form of terrorism. You don't generally get through it unscathed. Right now the concern is your physical safety, but when it's over you can't overlook your emotional well-being."

"You spend a lot of time evaluating your emotional well-being, Zach?"

"Believe it or not, they don't let you in or out of the FBI without a psych eval. Same goes for in and out of undercover work—and a few of those messed me up enough to require some therapy. Talking to someone doesn't scare me, and it shouldn't scare you."

"That hardly scares me."

But the way she scoffed, he wasn't so sure. Still, it was none of his business. Her recovery was not part of keeping her safe, and the latter was all he was supposed to care about.

"Let's talk about the people on this list," Zach said, pushing the computer screen toward her. On the screen was a list of people she'd told her brother she thought might want to hurt her.

Daisy rubbed her temples. "Vaughn gave you this?"

He rose, retrieved some aspirin from the cabinet above the sink and set it next to her elbow. "Your brother gave me copies of everything pertaining to the stalking."

Daisy frowned at the aspirin bottle, then up at him. "Am I supposed to tip you?"

"Full service security and investigation, Ms. Delaney. Speaking of that, Delaney's a stage name, isn't it?"

"What? You don't have a full dossier on my real name and everything else?" She smirked at him.

He shook his head. The Delaney connection wasn't important. As unimportant as the way that smirk made his gut tighten with a desire he would never, *ever* act on.

What was important was her take on the list and what kind of patterns and conclusions he could draw. So he turned the conversation back to the case and made sure it stayed there.

# Chapter Three

Sleep was a welcome relief from worry, except when the dreams came. They didn't always make sense, but Tom's lifeless body always appeared.

Even hiking up the mountains at sunset. It was peaceful, and Zach was with her, smiling. She liked his smile, and she liked the riot of sunset colors in the sky. She wanted to write a song, itched to.

Suddenly, she had a notebook and a pen, but when she started to write it became a picture of Tom, and then she tripped and it was Tom's body. She reached out for Zach's help, but it was only Tom's lifeless eyes staring back from Zach's face.

She didn't know whether she was screaming or crying, maybe it was both, and then she fell with a jolt. Her eyes flew open, face wet and breath coming so fast it hurt her lungs.

Somehow, she knew Zach was standing

there. It didn't even give her a start. It seemed right and steadying that he was standing in her doorway in nothing but a pair of sweatpants, a dim glow from the room behind him.

Later, she'd give some considerable thought to just how *cut* Zach was, all strong arms and abs. Something else he hid quite well, and she was sure quite purposefully.

"You screamed and you didn't lock your door," he offered, slowly lowering the gun to his side. He looked up at the ceiling, and gestured toward her. "You might want to…"

He trailed off and in her jumble of emotions and dream confusion, it took her a good minute to realize the strap of her tank top had fallen off her arm and she was all but flashing him.

She wasn't embarrassed so much as tired. Bone-deep tired of how this whole thing was ruining her life. "Sorry," she grumbled, fixing the shirt and pulling the sheet up around her.

"No. That's not…" He cleared his throat. "You should lock that door."

She wished she could find amusement in his obvious discomfort over being flashed a little breast, but she was too tired. "Lock the door to shield myself from lunatics with guns?" she asked, nodding at the pistol he carried.

"To take precautions," he said firmly.

"Are you telling me if I'd screamed and the door had been locked you wouldn't have busted in here, guns blazing?"

"They were hardly blazing," he returned, ignoring the question.

But she knew the answer. She might not know or understand Zach Simmons, but he had that same thing her brother did. A dedication to whatever he saw as his mission.

Currently, she was Zach Simmons's mission. She wished it gave her any comfort, but with Tom's dead face flashing in her mind, she didn't think anything could.

"You want a drink?" he asked, and despite that bland tone he used with such effectiveness, the offer was kind.

"Yes. Yes, I do."

He nodded. "I'll see what I can scrounge up. You can meet me out there."

She took that as a clear hint to put on some decent clothes. On a sigh, she got out of bed and rifled through her duffel bag. She pulled out her big, fluffy robe in bright yellow. It made her feel a little like Big Bird, which always made her smile.

Tonight was an exception, but it at least gave her something sunny to hold on to as she stepped out of the room. Zach was pouring whiskey into a shot glass. He'd pulled on a T-shirt, but it wasn't the kind of shirt he'd worn yesterday that hid all that surprisingly solid muscle. No, it fit him well, and allowed her another bolt of surprisingly intense attraction.

He set the shot glass on the table and gestured her into the seat. She slid into it, staring at the amber liquid somewhat dubiously. "Thanks." But she didn't shoot it. She just stared at it. "Got anything to put it in? I may love a song about shooting whiskey, but honestly shots make me gag."

His mouth quirked, but he nodded, pulling a can of pop out of the fridge.

"No diet?"

"I'll put it on the grocery list."

"And where does one get groceries in the middle of nowhere Wyoming?"

"Believe it or not, even Wyomingites need to eat. I've got an assistant who'll take care of errands. If you make a list, we'll supply."

She sipped the drink he put in front of her. The mix of sugar and whiskey was a comforting familiarity in the midst of all this... upheaval.

"You don't shoot whiskey."

She quirked a smile at him. "Not all my songs are autobiographical, friend. Truth be told, I'd prefer a beer, but it doesn't give you quite the same buzz, does it?"

"No, but I'd think more things would rhyme with beer than whiskey."

"Songs also don't have to rhyme. Fancy yourself a country music expert? Or just a Daisy Delaney expert?"

"No expertise claimed. I studied up on your work, not that I hadn't heard it before. Some of your songs make a decent showing on the radio."

"Decent. Don't get that Jordan Jones airtime, but who does? Certainly no one with breasts." This time she didn't sip. She took a good, long pull. Silly thing to be peeved about Jordan's career taking off while hers seemed to level. Bigger things at hand. Nightmares, dead bodyguards, empty Wyoming towns.

"The police don't suspect him."

She took another long drink. "No, they don't."

"Do you?"

She stared at the bubbles popping at the surface of her soda. Did she think the man she'd married with vows of faith and love and certainty was now stalking her? That he killed the person in charge of keeping her safe?

"I don't want to."

"But you think he could be responsible?" Zach pressed. Clearly, he didn't care if he was pressing on an open, gaping wound.

"I doubt it. But I wouldn't put it past one of his people. After I filed for divorce they did a number on me. Fake stories about cheating and drinking and unstable behavior, and before you point it out, no, my songs did not help me in that regard. Funny how my daddy was *revered* for those types of songs, even when he left Mama high and dry, but me? I'm a crazy floozy who deserves what she gets."

Zach's gaze was placid and blank, lacking all judgment. She didn't have a clue why that pissed her off, but it did. So she drank deeply, waiting for that warm tingle to spread. Hopefully slow down the whirring in her brain a little bit. "I don't want to have a debate about feminism or gender equality. I want to be safe home in my own bed. And I want Tom to be alive."

"I'm working on one of those. I'm sorry I can't fix the rest."

He said it so blankly. No emotion behind it at all, and yet this time it soothed her. Because she believed those words so much more without someone trying to *act* sincere.

"What did you dream about?" he asked as casual and devoid of emotion as he'd been this whole time.

Except when he'd been uncomfortable about her wandering breast. She held on to the fact that Mr. Ex-FBI man could be a little thrown off.

"Hiking. You. Tom. It's a jumble of nonsense, and not all that uncommon for me. I've always had vivid dreams, bad ones when I'm…well, bad. They've just never been so connected or relentless."

"I imagine your life has never been so relentless and threatening."

"Fair."

"The dreams aren't fun, but they'll be there. Meditation works for some. Alcohol for others, though I wouldn't make that one a habit. Exercise and wearing yourself out works, too."

"Let me guess, that's your trick?"

He shrugged. "I've done all three."

"Your job gave you dreams?"

"Yeah. Dreams are your subconscious, the things you often can't or don't deal with awake. It's your brain trying to work through it all when you can't outthink it."

"You've given brains a *lot* more thought than I ever have."

"There's a psychology to undercover work. Your work deals with the heart more than the brain."

Because he cut to the quick of her entire life's vocation a little too easily, and it smoothed over jagged edges in a way she didn't understand, she chose to focus on the other part of the sentence.

"You went undercover? Yeah, I can see that. Bring down any big guns?"

He shrugged. "Here and there."

"What's the point if you're not going to brag about it?"

He pondered that, then gave his answer with utter conviction. "Justice. Satisfaction."

She wrinkled her nose. "I'd prefer a little limelight."

"I suppose that's why I'm in security, and you're in entertainment."

"I suppose." She finished the drink. She wasn't really sure what had mellowed her mood more—the buzz or Zach's conversation. She had a sinking suspicion it was both, and that he was aware of that. "I guess I'll try to sleep now. I appreciate the…" She didn't know what to call it—from responding to her distress to a simple drink and conversation— it was more than she'd been given in…a long time.

Well, if she was fair, more than she'd allowed herself. And that had started a heck of a lot longer ago than the stalking.

She stood, never finishing her sentence. Zach stood, as well, cleaning up her mess. For some reason that didn't sit right, but she didn't do anything to remedy it. She opened the door to her bedroom, took one last glance back at him.

He was heading for his own door. A strange mystery of a man with a very good heart under all that blankness.

He paused at his door. He didn't look at her, but she had no doubt he knew she was looking at him.

"Daisy." It might have been the first time he'd said her name, or maybe it was just the first time he'd said her name where it sounded human to human. So she waited, breath held for who knew what reason.

"You've been through a lot. It isn't just losing someone you feel responsible for losing. You've uprooted your life, changed everything around you. You might be used to life on the road, but this is different. You don't have your singing outlet. So give yourself a break."

With that, he stepped into his room, the door closing and locking behind him.

ZACH DIDN'T NEED much sleep on a normal day, but even with the usual four hours under his belt, he felt a little rough around the edges the next morning. He supposed it had to do with them being interrupted by Daisy's screaming.

It had damn near scared a year off his life.

Any questions or doubts he'd had were gone, though. Someone or something was terrorizing her. Didn't mean he wouldn't look at cold, hard facts. Hadn't he learned what getting too emotionally involved in a case got you?

Yeah, he was susceptible to vulnerability. He could admit that now. Being plagued by dreams, by guilt over the man who'd died only for taking a job protecting her, it all added up to vulnerable.

And he was *not* thinking about the slip of her top because that had nothing to do with anything.

He grunted his way through push-ups, sit-ups, lunges and squats. He'd need to bring a few more things from home. Maybe just move it all. He wasn't planning on spending much time back in Cheyenne with his business here.

His room still needed a lot of work, and he'd get to it once this case was shored up— as long as he didn't immediately have another one. Still, he had a floor, a rudimentary bathroom and a bed. What more did a guy need?

He knew his mother worried about him throwing too much into his job, whether because she feared he'd suffer the same fate as his father—murdered in revenge for the work he'd done as an ATF agent—or because she just worried about him having more of a life than work, it didn't matter.

He liked his work. It fulfilled him. Besides, he had friends. Cousins, actually. Finding his long-lost sister meant finding his mother's family, and he might get along more with the people they'd married, but it was still camaraderie.

He had a full life.

But he sat there on the floor of a ramshackle room, sweating from the brief workout, and wondered at the odd pang of longing for something he couldn't name. Something he'd never had until he'd met his sister—of course that had coincided with being officially fired from the FBI, so maybe it was more that than the other.

It didn't matter. Because not only was he *fine*, he also had a job to do.

He could hear Daisy stirring out in the common room. Coffee or breakfast or both, if he had to guess.

He'd hoped she'd sleep longer because there were some areas he wanted to press on today, and he'd likely back off if she looked tired.

Or he could suck it up and be a hard-ass, which was what this job called for, wasn't it? He knew what being soft got him, so he needed to steel his determination to be hard.

He ran through a cold shower, got dressed, grabbed his computer and stepped out to find Daisy in the kitchen.

She was dressed in tight jeans and a neon-pink T-shirt that read *Straight Shooter* in sparkly sequins on the back. On the sleeve of each arm was a revolver outline in more sequins. When she turned from the oven where she was scrambling some eggs, she flashed a smile.

Her hair was pulled back to reveal bright green cactus earrings, and she'd put on makeup. Dark eyes, bright lips.

The fact she'd made herself up, looked like she could step on stage in the snap of her fingers, he assumed she was hiding a rough night under all that polish.

But the polish helped him pretend, too.

"Want some?" she asked, tipping the pan toward him.

"Sure, if you've got enough." He dropped the laptop off on the table and then moved toward her to get plates, but she waved him away.

"You waited on me yesterday. My turn. Besides, I familiarized myself this morning. Thanks for making coffee, by the way. Good stuff."

"Programmable machine," he returned, not

sure what to do with himself while she took care of breakfast. He opted for getting himself a cup of coffee.

He didn't want to loom behind her, so he took a seat at the table and opened his laptop. He booted up his email to see if there were any more reports from Ranger Cooper, but nothing.

She slid a plate in front of him, then took the seat opposite him with her own plate.

"So, what's the deal? Play house in here until they figure out who did it?" she asked with just a tad too much cheer in her voice—clearly trying to compensate for the edge she felt.

"Partially. We're working on a protected outdoor area, but staying inside for now is best." He tapped his computer. "It gives us time to work through who might be after you."

She wrinkled her nose. "Believe it or not, sifting through who might hate me enough to hurt me isn't high on my want-to-do list."

"But I assume going home, getting back to your family and your career is. Lesser of two evils."

She ate, frowning. But she didn't try to argue, and he was going to do his job today. Nightmares and vulnerability couldn't stop the job.

"I want to talk about your ex."

"So does everyone," she muttered.

"Your divorce was news?" he asked, even though he'd known it was. Much as he didn't keep up with pop culture, he'd seen enough magazines at the checkout counter with her face and her ex's.

"Yeah. I mean, maybe not if you don't pay attention to country music, but Jordan had really started to make a name for himself with crossovers. So the story got big. And I got crucified."

"Why didn't he?" Zach asked casually, taking a bite of the eggs, which were perfectly cooked.

"Because he's perfect?"

"You wanted to divorce him," he pointed out. "He can't be perfect. No one is."

"Or that's exactly why I wanted to divorce him."

He studied her. The lifted chin, the challenge in her eyes. "Yeah, I don't buy that."

Her shoulders slumped. "Yeah, our families didn't, either. Neither did he, for that matter. I don't know how to explain… Do we really have to discuss my very public divorce?"

"Yeah. We really do. The more I understand, the better I can find the pattern."

"And if it's not him?"

"Then the pattern won't say it is."

"People aren't patterns, Zach. They're not always rational, or sane."

"Yeah, I'm well aware, but routine stalkers are methodical. It's not a moment of rage. It's not knee-jerk or impulse. It's planned terrorizing. Murder of your bodyguard? There was no struggle. It was planned. This person is methodical, which means if I can figure out their methodology, I can figure this out."

She heaved out a sigh. "You believe that."

"I know that."

"Fine. Fine. Why did I file for divorce against Jordan? I don't know. It's complicated. It's all emotions and… Did your parents love each other?"

Unconcerned with the abrupt change, because every thread led him somewhere, he nodded. "Very much."

"Mine didn't. Or maybe they did, but it was warped. It hurt."

He thought about his brother, alone in a psych ward, still lost to whatever had taken a hold of his mind. "Love often does."

"You got someone?"

"Not romantically."

"Family, then?"

He nodded.

"I used to think loving my brother didn't

hurt, not even a little—not the way loving my father did, or even my mom. Vaughn was perfect, and always did the right thing. He protected me and loved me unconditionally. But this hurts, thinking he could be in danger because of me."

"He's a Texas Ranger."

"That doesn't make him invincible. He also has a wife and two little girls and…" She swallowed, looking away from him. "I can't…"

"The best thing for 'I can't' is figuring this out. Looking at the patterns, and finding who's at the center."

"You really think you can do that?"

"I do. With your help."

She nodded. "Okay. Okay. Well, sit back and relax, cowboy. The story of Daisy Delaney and Jordan Jones is a long one."

He lifted the coffee mug to his lips to try and hide his smile. "We've got nothing but time, Daisy."

# Chapter Four

"We met at a party." It was still so clear in Daisy's head. She'd stepped outside for air, and he'd followed. He'd complimented her on her music—never once mentioning her daddy.

She'd been a little too desperate for that kind of compliment at the time. She'd made a name for herself, but only when that name directly followed her father's.

"And this was before any of Jordan's success?"

Zach sat there, poised over his computer like he'd type it all out. Jot down her entire marriage in a few pithy lines and then find some magical *pattern* that either found Jordan culpable or…not.

"My brother looked into Jordan, you know."

"Yes, I know. I have all the information he gathered in regards to the…let's call it *external stuff*. But there's a lot of internal stuff I doubt you shared with your brother."

She laughed. "But you think I'll share it with a complete stranger?"

Zach blew out a breath, and though he had to be irritated with her, it didn't really show in the ways she was *used* to people being irritated with her.

"I know this is personal," Zach said, all calm and even and perfectly civil. "It hurts to mine through all these old things you thought were normal parts of a normal life. I'm not trivializing what you might feel, Daisy. I'm trying to understand someone's motivation for stalking and terrorizing you, and murdering your bodyguard."

"So you can find your precious pattern?" she asked, her throat too tight to sound as callous as she wanted to sound.

"Yeah, the precious pattern that might save your life."

She wanted to lean her head against the table and weep. Somehow, she had no doubt Zach would be kind and discreet about it, and it made her perversely more determined to keep it together. "He was sweet, and attentive. We had a lot in common, though he'd grown up on some hoity-toity, well-to-do Georgia farm and I'd grown up on the road. Still, the way he talked about music and his career made sense to me. He made sense to me. He asked me to marry him assuring me that it didn't have to change my career—because he knew where my priorities were."

"So you married for love?"

"Isn't that why people get married?"

"People get married for all sorts of reasons, I think. In your case, you've got fame and money on your side."

"Are you suggesting Jordan married me for my fame and money?"

"No, I'm asking if he did."

"I didn't think so." Even after she'd asked for a divorce, she hadn't thought Jordan could be that cold and manipulative, but after everything that had happened since the divorce... "He was so careful about any work we did together. Had to make sure it was the right project. He didn't insinuate himself into my career. So it didn't seem that way..."

"But?"

She didn't like the way he seemed to understand where her thoughts were going. She was clearly telegraphing all her feelings, and Zach was too observant. She needed to pull her masks together.

"He didn't fight me on the divorce. We'd grown apart. He'd thrown everything into his tour, his album, and I was touring and... We were both sort of bitter with each other but couldn't talk about it. I said we should end it and he agreed. He agreed. So simple, so smooth. Everything that came after was…calculated. Careful. He wanted us to split award shows."

"Huh?"

"Like choose which award shows we'd attend. If he was going to be at one, I wouldn't be. Like they were holidays you split the kids between. I don't know. I remember when my parents got divorced, it was screaming matches and throwing things and drunkenness. Not…paperwork."

"So it was amicable?"

Daisy hesitated. She'd dug her own grave, so to speak, with some of her behavior after she'd asked for the divorce. Because when he'd politely accepted her request and immediately obtained the necessary paperwork, she'd been…

Sometimes she tried to convince herself her pride had been injured, but the truth was she'd been devastated. She'd thrown out divorce as an option to get some kind of reaction out of him, to ignite a spark like they'd had before they'd gotten married.

But he'd gone along. Agreed. Wanted custody agreements over *award shows*.

So she hadn't handled herself well. At all.

She'd never imagined *this*. She'd only acted out her hurt and anger and betrayal the best way she knew how.

Breaking stuff and getting drunk.

"*He* was amicable, I guess you could say. I was...less so."

"But you were the one who asked for the divorce."

"Yes." As much as she didn't want to get into this with Zach, she supposed she'd end up giving him whatever information he thought might help with his precious patterns. What else was there to do? How else did she survive this?

"Yes, because I wanted him to fight for me, or be mad at me or react to me in some way. But he didn't. I started thinking he'd never loved me, because he was so calm. If there'd been love, it would have gone bitter. Mine did. I think he just used me for as long as I'd let him, then was happy to move on." As if it had been his plan all along.

Even now, a year later, the stab of pain that went along with that was hard to swallow down or rationalize away.

There were bigger tragedies in the world than a failed marriage, including her dead bodyguard.

"So maybe it could be Jordan, but if it is

him, it's not because I divorced him. Trust me, he got everything he wanted and *more* out of that situation. I don't think he'd sully his precious reputation by slapping back at me, when the press did all the work eviscerating me for him."

"Okay. What about other exes?"

"Because only a jilted lover could be after me?"

"Because we're going through the rational options first. We'll move to the irrational crazed fan angle after—" The sound of a phone trilling cut him off.

He pulled his cell out of his pocket, glanced at the display, then answered. "Yeah?" His face changed. She couldn't have described how. A tensing, maybe? Suddenly, there was more of an edge to him. The blandness sharpened into something that made her stomach tighten with a little bit of fear, and just a touch of very inappropriate lust.

If only she knew how to be appropriate.

He fired off questions like *when?* and *description?* jotting down what she assumed were the answers on the back of one of the many pieces of paper in the file.

"Get what you can for me," he said tersely and hung up.

He jotted a few more things down then got

to his feet like he was going to walk off to his room without saying anything.

"What was that?" Daisy demanded, hating the hint of hysteria in her voice.

"Just some updates. Nothing to worry about."

She fairly leaped out of her chair and grabbed his arm before he could disappear into his room.

He clearly didn't know her very well because he raised a condescending eyebrow, like that would have her moving her hand. But she'd be damned if she was letting go until she said what she had to say. "You want me safe? I have to know what's going on."

"That isn't necessarily true," he replied in that bland tone of his. "Knowing doesn't do much. All you have to do is stay put. I'll be back."

"You'll be back? You don't honestly expect me to—"

"I expect you to listen to the man currently keeping you safe. Do me a favor? Don't be cliché or stupid. Which means stay put. I'll be back." And then he walked out the front door.

And locked it from the outside.

ZACH HAD NO doubt he'd made all the wrong moves in there, but he didn't have time to make the right ones. He pocketed his keys, double-checked the gun holstered to his side and stepped out into daylight.

He took a deep breath of the fresh air, trying not to feel the prick of guilt at Daisy being locked inside for close to twenty-four hours. But it was for her safety, and Cam's phone call proved to him that he had to keep being excessively vigilant.

Which was why he scowled when Cam pulled up to the shack that disguised a garage behind the big house. Hilly was in the passenger seat so Zach tried to fix his expression into something neutral, but his sister being here complicated things.

Hilly was acting as their assistant. She ran the errands for groceries and the like, and she was helping with some of the paperwork while she went through nursing school.

Cam pulled his truck into the garage, then he and Hilly exited. Zach pushed the button himself to close the door so it went back to looking like a falling-down shack.

Cam's expression grave and Hilly's suspicious. "I still can't believe this place," she said with a little shudder. "It's so *creepy* from the outside."

Zach smiled thinly. "And, as you well know,

perfectly livable from the inside. So what's the deal?"

"Is she in there?" Hilly asked with a frown.

"Yeah."

"Well, let's go inside."

Zach rocked back on his heels. "Not a great idea right now. Besides, she doesn't need to know about this."

Hilly's frown deepened. Zach wanted to scowl at Cam for bringing her, but that would only make Hilly angrier.

Truth be told, he didn't understand the way Hilly got angry at all. It was sneaky, and came at you in new and confusing ways. Like guilt. He didn't care for it.

She glanced back at Cam. "I thought I was here to see what Daisy needed."

"You are," Cam agreed. "I just have some things I need to discuss with Zach about the case privately. I thought maybe I could do that while you talk to Daisy about anything she might need."

She looked back at Zach, her lips pursed, surveying him. An expression he never knew how to fully read. Judgment? Disappointment?

"I still think we can go inside and talk. There are rooms. Or you can let me go inside while you two powwow out here."

*Nicole Helm* 65

"Aren't you going to demand to know what's going on?"

"No. Cam and I agreed that there were certain cases that required his confidentiality. I'm okay with that. So why don't you let me in?"

Zach nodded. He didn't particularly want to introduce anyone to Daisy, but she was likely tired of just *him* and walls for company. Hilly could talk to her about anything she needed, maybe make her feel a little more at home, and Cam could fill him in on the details in the privacy of his room.

They walked to the front of the house and Zach unlocked and relocked doors as they entered, and when he stepped into the common area he frowned at the absence of Daisy.

Then at the fact the door to his room was open. He stepped toward it, hand moving to his gun without fully thinking the move through.

He stopped short in the doorway, shock and irritation clawing through him at equal measure. "What the hell do you think you're doing?" Zach demanded from the doorway.

Daisy didn't even have the decency to jump as she sat there on his bed, rifling through his things.

"I can't say your room holds any deep, dark surprises, Zach. Bland guy. Bland... Oh, hello." Daisy leaned her head to the side to look around him.

"Get your hands off my stuff."

She blinked up at him oh so innocently. "Won't you be doing the same for me? Or have you already?" She got to her feet in a fluid movement and crossed to Hilly and Cam and held out her hand.

"Daisy Delaney," she offered with a sassy grin that likely served her well on stage.

"Hi, I'm Hilly," Hilly said eagerly, shaking Daisy's hand. "I'm Zach's sister."

"Zach's sister." Daisy looked at him and raised an eyebrow before her smile sharpened. "Well, Hilly, you might be my new best friend."

"Sorry, if you're looking for dirt we only kind of found out about each other last year."

"Okay, so you can't give me the Zach dirt. How about you tell me what the hell is going on? I'm presuming you know." She moved her gaze to Cam. "Or you do."

"I, uh…" Cam cleared his throat, looking shockingly ruffled and uncomfortable.

"He's a big fan," Hilly stage-whispered.

"I am not," Cam retorted, sounding downright strangled. "I mean, I *am*, but not… Oh, hell."

Hilly laughed, leaning into Cam. They were

more of a unit than Zach would ever be with his own sister, and he was never quite sure what to do with that sick wave of jealousy that swamped him sometimes.

Hilly had been kidnapped and raised as someone else. What would he envy of her life?

But when she linked hands with Cam and talked excitedly to Daisy, he knew exactly what.

"Hilly, why don't you take Daisy out to the kitchen and get her list. Hilly's our assistant. She can run any errands you need."

"Oh, he's dismissing the womenfolk," Daisy said with a sweetness that went bitter at the edges.

Zach could tell Hilly was trying to suppress a smile. But she didn't fight him. "I'm sure there are some things you'd like to have, Ms. Delaney. I can get you whatever you need."

"Call me Daisy," she replied, heading for the door with Hilly.

Zach *knew* he should keep his mouth shut, let it go. But she downright needled him. "We'll talk about you going through my stuff later," he muttered as she passed.

"Ooh, shaking in my boots, baby cakes."

He sneered, as irritated with himself for letting her get to him as he was at her for being obnoxious as hell.

"Things are going well, then," Cam offered once Daisy and Hilly disappeared into the common room.

"Things are going fine. I want the full report."

"We didn't catch him at the airport, but a man was quizzing Jen at the General Store. Get many strangers, etc. She gave me a call and I ran him. Came in on a flight from Texas, but after Daisy's. No connections yet, but probably more than a coincidence. Someone's following her."

"I want to know *how*."

"Don't you want to know who?"

"Maybe. But if this is the stalker, they suddenly got so dumb they're sniffing around a small town thinking they won't make waves. My money's on a plant, or a hired hand. The *how* is more relevant than the *who*."

"He's rented a room in Fairmont, but I have some suspicions that's to throw us off."

"Does he know about *us*?"

"Unclear. As far as I can tell, he only has a vague idea of where she is. I assume he knows she's under some kind of protection, but he didn't make Hilly or me, and nobody followed us out here."

"We took every precaution." But something hadn't worked. Something had gotten through.

"It happens, Zach. Now we focus on protecting her. Jen's getting together her security footage and I'll work on an ID and any connections to Daisy. I'm sure you'll obsess over a pattern. Bottom line, we'll keep her safe."

Except hadn't he already failed at that? Maybe she was safe *now*, but the threat was at her door just like it had been back in Texas.

"Hey," Cam said. "Nothing's ever going to go according to plan. You know that."

Zach nodded at Cam. But a mistake had been made—plans or no plans—and that mistake had to be figured out before the consequences of his mistake started knocking.

## Chapter Five

Daisy liked Hilly. She hadn't thought she would when the young woman had ushered her out of Zach's room with only a mild display of amusement.

But Hilly was sweet, a little heavy on the earnestness, which Daisy could only find endearing. The fact she'd ask for Daisy's autograph to give to the man huddled in Zach's room appealed to both Daisy's ego and the idea that love didn't always have to be messy. Hilly clearly loved her boyfriend and wasn't miffed that he'd gone a little tongue-tied over Daisy.

"So you don't know what's going on with the caveman clutch in there?" Daisy asked, scowling at Zach's door as Hilly finished up the list. It would be nice to have some *real* food in this place.

Hilly smiled. "They aren't really. Cavemen, that is. They're just...serious."

Which didn't answer the question. "No offense, Hilly, but one's your brother and one's your…" She trailed off, glanced at the rock on Hilly's hand. Not bad taste for a caveman, but Hilly could have picked it out herself. "Fiancé. You're not an unbiased observer."

"I suppose not, but they're good men. They both helped save me from people who wanted to hurt me."

"Really?"

"Zach's saved a lot of people, and gotten himself hurt in the process more than once. He's a good man. That I can promise you."

Hilly smiled as Cam and Zach stepped out of Zach's room, looking just as Hilly had described them: serious.

"I'll tell you about it sometime. Or ask Zach."

"Ask me what?"

Hilly shook her head and stood, slipping the list into her pocket. "I should head out to get the supplies so I can get them back to you before dinner."

"I'll keep in touch," Cam said to Zach.

"Aren't you going to say goodbye to Daisy, Cam?" Hilly asked sweetly.

He glared at her but then offered Daisy a smile and a nod. "It was nice to meet you, Ms. Delaney," he offered stiffly.

"Call me Daisy, sweetheart."

Cam made a little noise that might have been a squeak if he wasn't so tall and broad. Hilly ushered him out and that left her with Zach.

She scowled at him. Truth be told, she should be used to overly serious men worrying a little too much about her safety, but she'd always managed to keep Vaughn on the fringe of all that. Travel and no real trouble had helped until the past year.

But regardless of Vaughn's interference in her life, she wasn't used to someone being all up in her business. She wasn't used to someone getting under her skin in such a short amount of time.

And none of it mattered, because at the end of the day, her irritation with Zach didn't matter. Getting through this mattered. "I want to know what's going on."

"And I want to know why you were rifling through my stuff," he retorted, a slash of temper barely leashed.

Was it wrong she liked temper on him? That he wasn't all Mr. Bland Stoic? Because *this* was a lot more enjoyable than his pat, crap answers. So she grinned at him, since it seemed to make him grind his teeth together. "Show me yours, I'll show you mine."

"Someone followed you."

It took any and all enjoyment out of the moment. She sank into the chair when her legs went a little wobbly. "What?"

"Someone followed you here," Zach said, his voice flat but his eyes flashing with anger.

Was it at her or whoever was here? She wasn't sure she wanted to know.

"So I need a list of everyone who knew you were coming."

"You know the list," she replied, trying to keep the tremor out of her voice. "You, Jaime and my brother. Hate to break it to you, but they're not high on my suspect list. Well, I don't know you. It could be you."

"You didn't tell anyone that you were going out of town, or post a picture from the airport or—"

Injured pride reignited her irritation. "Oh, screw you."

"Hey, someone is *here*, and now I have to keep you safe under an even bigger threat, so a little truthfulness would be nice."

"Because I'm such a liar?"

"Get it through your thick, obnoxious skull that your pride doesn't matter right now. One person, any person, who might have known you were leaving town, heading to the airport, anything. Because it matters. Clearly, if someone is here looking for you, it matters."

It was on the tip of her tongue to immediately dismiss him. But…it wouldn't be true, and she wanted to be safe more than she wanted to be righteous.

Just barely.

"I… I told my manager I was going to Wyoming, but—"

"Of all the idiotic bull—"

"I trust Stacy with my *life*," she shot back before he could finish. "I trust her with everything. It isn't her."

"Okay, great. So the three people who knew you were coming to Wyoming were your brother, an FBI agent and your manager. Who spilled the beans?"

"Maybe *you* did, jerk."

"Sure. I'm a security professional, but I bragged about bagging a big star client to someone who has a connection to you."

"I don't know you! You could have."

"But I know me, and I didn't. Stacy… Stacy Vine. That's your manager, right?"

"You cannot look into her."

"Can. Will."

She would not be so weak as to cry. She'd save that for when he couldn't see and lord it over her later. But her voice wasn't nearly strong enough. "You're asking me which of these people I *love* wants me dead."

He softened. She saw it all over his face and wanted to hate him for it. It would be easier if he was just the overbearing jerk, but he offered empathy far too often for it to be that simple.

God, she wanted something, anything, to be simple.

He took one of the chairs and moved it across from her. He sat, facing her, so that their knees were almost touching. He leaned forward, and she found herself wanting to lean forward, too. Wanting to be touched, comforted.

Wasn't that a joke? She knew better on a good day, with a man who actually liked her. This was neither of those things.

"It doesn't have to be that cut-and-dried. She could have mentioned it to an assistant. Written it down and someone read it. This is why the *who* is important, Daisy. If it's someone who's got a personal tie to you, they might be stalking people you know and love, too."

"How many ways do you want to hurt me, Zach?" She held up a hand before he could answer. He wasn't trying to hurt her. He had a job to do, protection to see to. Anything that hurt was all hers. "Sorry. That wasn't fair."

"You don't have to be fair. I'm going to do my job no matter what you are. Be mad, be unfair, but I need the truth. Always. It's the only way we get you out of this."

*We.* Like they were some kind of team. Which was too much the story of her life. Thinking some man was in it for her—Dad, Jordan—only to find all they cared about was their own bottom line. She didn't know how to weather that again.

What other option was there? She could lie to him, not trust him, and where did it get her? Nowhere. She was in the hardest lose-lose situation of her entire life, and boy, was that saying something.

"She's the only one aside from Vaughn and Jaime that knows. Nat—that's Vaughn's wife—might know, but Vaughn's pretty by-the-book. Even if he told her, he'd swear her to secrecy, and Nat would listen. You could always ask them, but I doubt they'd be careless."

"So we'll look into your manager."

"Yeah, sure. Fantastic."

Zach sighed, then rested his hand over hers. Warm, strong, capable. She really wanted to hate him, and he made it so dang hard.

"One thing at a time, okay? And eventually, we'll get there."

It was a cliché, and stupid, and worst of all, it made her feel better.

ZACH SPENT MOST of his day looking into the manager, her connections and trying to figure out how anyone had followed Daisy here.

It couldn't be cut-and-dried because the person didn't know *exactly* where Daisy was, so that made any patterns sketchy at best. A frustrating point of fact Zach was having trouble accepting.

He also spent considerable time checking his security measures and watching the footage of the security cameras he had positioned on different places outside the house. When he was half convinced he saw a tumbleweed pass across his deserted Main Street he knew it was time to do something else.

Still, no matter what he did or how little he interacted with Daisy, he could practically feel the stir-crazy coming off her.

When Hilly returned with the groceries, and some updates on the tasks he'd asked her to accomplish, Zach thanked her and sent her away, though it was clear she wanted to stay and chat.

Much as Zach trusted Hilly and Cam to be aware of anyone following them, he didn't want to take too many chances on comings and goings being noticed—whether by the wrong people or even by locals who might talk.

Armed with the special item he'd tasked Hilly to find, Zach went to Daisy's room. She'd been inside with the door closed for about an hour. He knew she wasn't sleeping because he could hear her moving around.

He knocked, feeling stupid and determined in equal measure. It wasn't his job to set Daisy at ease or make her comfortable, but it wasn't *not* his job, either.

She opened the door with that haughty, bad-girl smirk, though it couldn't hide the wariness in her gaze. Still, both smirk and wariness softened as she noticed what he held in his hands.

"A guitar," she breathed, like he was holding a leprechaun's pot of gold.

"I don't know much about music, but there's a music shop in Fairmont and Hilly stopped in and picked one up. Probably not the quality you're used to, but—"

"Hilly stopped in and picked one up or you asked her to?"

"Does it matter?"

She tilted her head, studying him. In the end, she didn't say anything. She took the offered guitar and slid her fingers over the wood, the strings, the body and the arm.

There was something a little too erotic about watching her do that so he moved into the kitchen. It wasn't quite dinnertime yet, but they could certainly eat. If only to keep him from embarrassing himself.

But he couldn't quite seem to keep his gaze off the way she stroked the instrument, which meant he had to say something. *Do* something. Anything to keep his mind out of places he couldn't let it wander.

"I get a free concert, right?"

She grinned, turning the guitar over in her hands. She slid the strap over her shoulder, picked at the strings, fiddled with the knobs and whatever else.

"Ain't nothing free in this life, sugar." She said it, and then she sang it, noodling into one of her father's songs. The relaxation in her was nearly immediate. She softened, eased and lost herself in the song.

It was…enchanting, which wasn't a word he'd ever used or probably even thought, but she was mesmerizing. Like a fairy. With a dark, mischievous side. She moved seamlessly from one of her father's raucous drinking songs to one of her newer ones—the one she'd had some success with right before her bodyguard had been killed.

Sadness crept into her features, but not fear. She moved into a song it took him a few chords to recognize as one of the few duets she'd ever recorded with her father.

She stopped abruptly halfway through the song. "Hell, I miss that old bastard," she muttered.

That was a sadness he understood, and it made it impossible not to try and soothe. "My father wasn't a bastard, but I know the feeling."

"Not around?"

"He was murdered."

"Well. Hell, Zach, ease me into it, why don't you. Murdered?"

Zach raised a shoulder, no idea what prompted him to share that information. Soothing was one thing, but volunteering details was another. Yet, they piled up and fell out of him at a rapid rate. "Risks of the job. He was in the ATF, investigating a dangerous group. A long time ago. It happens."

"It shouldn't."

Why that simple phrase touched him was more than beyond him. He'd had a lot of time to deal with his father's death, accepting it and the unfairness of life. He'd investigated his father's murder, made sure it didn't consume him like it had his brother. He'd come to terms. He'd dealt.

But it shouldn't happen. No. It shouldn't.

"Is that why you do this?" she asked, still fiddling with the guitar.

"No, but it's why I went into the FBI. I'm assuming your father is why you went into music."

"Yes and no." She played a few more chords, humming with them. "He pushed me into it, and I did it partly for him, because of him, but I did it partly because it's in me. The chords, the stories." She pinned him with a look. "I'd say the same is true for you. Your father's life pushed you into law enforcement, but there's something in you that fits it."

"You'd be surprised," he muttered. "What sounds good for dinner?"

"Whatever," she said, taking a seat at the table and still playing random chords on the guitar like they were a link to safety or comfort. "I guess you didn't find anything with Stacy."

"No. Cam's working on the identity of who's here, and I'll have a report tonight, along with some video I'll want you to take a look at."

"Who's here. Why do you say it like that?"

"Like what?"

"Like who's behind this and who's here might be two separate people."

Her worry was back. She gripped the guitar hard enough her knuckles went white.

Part of him wanted to lie to her, but that wouldn't do. That was letting himself get too emotionally invested. "It's certainly a possibility."

"So there could be two of them?"

"No, I'd say it's more likely someone hired."

"Like…a hit man?"

"Or just someone sent to find you. A lot of shady things are for hire out there. It'd be a way to ferret out your exact location without getting caught themselves."

"So even if you catch *this* guy, it won't mean you can connect them to the stalker?"

"Doesn't mean we can't, either. We don't know yet."

She rubbed at her chest. "I thought I knew how to deal with the unknown. You never know what's going to succeed or fail in music. I thought I would always just go with the flow, but if I hear you say we don't know one more time I might have a mental breakdown."

"Hey, this is the place for mental breakdowns. Creepy ghost town facade and all the modern comforts of home."

She laughed, but it faded quickly. "Home. Do you have a home?"

"I assume you mean home in the symbolic sense, not just four walls and a roof?"

"Bingo, cowboy."

Zach thought it over. Home to him was his grandparents' ranch they'd moved to after Dad had died. He'd never made one for himself. This place he was standing in meant something to him— bigger than just a building or a job—but it still wasn't...*home*.

"I guess not. I haven't really had anything permanent as an adult."

"I never had anything permanent."

"Do you ever wonder how you ended up the nomadic singer and your brother the stay-in-one-place Texas Ranger?"

"Are you just like your siblings?" she asked with one of her haughty raised eyebrows.

He sobered at the thought of his brother in a mental hospital, working through all the things that had twisted inside him since their father's death.

"You and Hilly seem similar," she offered as if *she* was trying to comfort *him*.

"Hilly and I only met just this year. I mean, I remember her when she was a baby, but—"

"She said the same thing. Add that to the

murdered father and I'd say you've got quite the story, Zach."

"She was kidnapped by the men who murdered my father and raised under a different name."

Daisy blinked and opened her eyes wide. "I'm sorry, *what?*"

He shrugged, uncomfortable both with the subject and his idiocy for discussing it. "It's complicated, but... Well, it's all figured out now."

"Does the calm, bland, bored facade ever get exhausting?"

He didn't care for how easily she saw through him, so he did his best to raise his eyebrow condescendingly like she did. "Who says it's a facade?"

Her mouth quirked up at one side. "You weren't so bland or bored when I was rifling through your stuff."

Even now the reminder made his jaw clench, even more so when she full-on grinned and pointed at him. "See? Underneath all that robot exterior, there is a man with a living, breathing heart." She looked down at the guitar in her lap and frowned. "Believe it or not, Zach, I'd rather have a man with a heart on this case over a robot. That's why I was going through your things. I wanted to see if I could get to that heart."

"Believe it or not, Daisy, I do what I have to do to keep you safe. Robot exterior included."

She pursed her lips together as if she didn't quite believe him. As if she took it as some kind of challenge.

Lucky for him, he was not a man to back down from a challenge any more than he was a man to lose one.

# Chapter Six

Zach was dead. Lifeless blue eyes. Blood everywhere. Just like Tom.

She turned to run, to save herself, but she tripped over another body and gasped out a sob.

Vaughn. *No.*

But even as she wanted to reach out, grab her brother, breathe some life into him, she ran. She didn't know how, because her brain was telling her running into the dark was all wrong.

But she kept running into the black. Into the danger.

"Daisy. Come on. Daisy." Zach's voice. But he was dead.

Still, she ran.

"Daisy. Stop."

She tried to speak, but she couldn't. She could only run and Zach swore viciously, the words echoing in the dark around her.

"Let's try this."

Why was Zach's voice haunting her? He was dead. She was alone. No, not alone. Running from...from who?

"Lucy?"

It wasn't immediate, but slowly she realized it wasn't totally pitch-black. A light glowed in the corner of the room. She smelled paint, not blood. And she could feel Zach there. Somehow she knew it was him, touching her shoulders.

"Lucy, wake up now."

Zach. Calling her by her real name. He was sitting on her bed. Twisted so that his hands gripped her shoulders, strong but gentle. He was using her real name and she was in Wyoming.

Dreaming.

"A dream," she muttered out loud.

"There now," he said, relief evident in his tone as he ran a hand down her spine. Weird to be comforted in a strange room with a man she barely knew touching her through the thin cotton of her pajamas.

But she *was* comforted. Enough that when he began to pull away she only leaned into him, ignoring the way his body stiffened. "You were dead. Vaughn was dead. And all I did was run."

His body softened against hers, and though his arms were more hesitant than take-control, he wrapped them around her.

A comfort hug. Maybe even a pity hug.

She didn't even care. She'd take comfort from pity if she had to. The images of that dream stuck with her, flashed in her head every time she closed her eyes. She focused on Zach instead.

He was warm with all that surprisingly hard muscle. He smelled like soap. She closed her eyes and breathed in deeply. She soaked in the warmth and rested her cheek against his chest, listening to his heartbeat.

A steady thump. As comforting as the rest of him.

She could feel his breath flutter the hair against her cheek. When he breathed, her body moved with the movement of his. Underneath her hands, splayed against his broad, strong back, she could feel his warmth seep into her.

What would all that muscle feel like without the Henley between her palms and his skin? To have her cheek pressed against his naked chest instead of soft cotton? She'd seen him with his shirt off. She could almost picture it.

So much better than the other pictures in her head.

It took her a minute to realize the buzz along her skin was pure, unadulterated *want*. And another minute to roll her eyes at herself for being so stupid and simple. She straightened, pulling away from him. His arms easily fell off her and he got to his feet quickly.

It amused her, soothed her a little, to think he might feel that bolt of attraction, too. What would be going on in that regimented brain of his?

"How about some ice cream?" he asked.

It made her smile. "Is sugar your answer to all of life's crises?"

"I wouldn't say sugar is the answer. Sugar is the…comfort. Besides, you had Hilly buy you some low-cal fruit atrocity kind. I figured you might be up for it."

"I'll take it." She slid out of bed. She'd learned her lesson that first night and had worn something acceptable to be seen in to bed.

Though, if she was honest with herself, she now regretted it. Thinking about an attraction to Zach, and what could be done about it when they were stuck in a weird safe house together, was far better than thinking about her dream or even her reality.

So she tried to decide what kind of come-on Zach Simmons, part robot, would respond to as she followed him out into the kitchen area. Nothing subtle. Being attracted to her was probably *very* against his personal code.

What would it take to make him break his personal code? She remembered the way he'd uncomfortably stared at the ceiling when her pajama top had been too revealing the other night. It made her laugh, which felt immeasurably good after the terror of that dream.

"Something funny?" he asked, looking at her with some concern—like maybe she'd lost it a little bit.

Maybe she had, but she figured she had a right to. "Just trying to think of things that make me laugh instead of cry or scream."

He frowned at that as he pulled out the carton of the frozen yogurt she'd requested. "I've been thinking about someone being here, and about what we can do."

"Thinking? Don't you sleep?"

He shrugged as he scooped the yogurt into the bowl. None for him, she noted. "When necessary."

When necessary. She had no idea why this man was such an endearing piece of work. Maybe it was because most of the men she knew pretended to have feelings when they really didn't, and Zach was the exact opposite.

"I think the leak is through your manager.

It's what makes the most sense anyway. So we pull on that." He set the bowl in front of her, then went back to the freezer and pulled out a different carton.

She stared at the sad bowl of low-fat fro-yo that sometimes tasted good enough to make her forget about ice cream. Less so when someone wanted her dead or traumatized or whatever.

"What does *pull on that* mean in cop speak?"

Zach slid into the chair next to her. The bowl of dark chocolate, full-fat ice cream he set in front of him made Daisy's mouth water.

"Send a few fake messages, see which ones get followed. I haven't worked it all out yet, but that's my thought, and I'll need you to do it."

"You want me to lie to Stacy?" Daisy asked, her stomach turning at the thought. She was a decent enough liar, what with being a performer and storyteller and all, but the idea of lying to Stacy to prove someone she loved and trusted was part of this nightmare...

Yeah, fro-yo wasn't going to cut it.

"They don't have to be lies. They just have to be leads. Something we can follow and see who picks it up."

It still sounded like lying to her, and it

sounded complicated. So she reached over and scooped a lump of his ice cream onto her spoon. Their eyes met as she slid the ice cream into her mouth.

It might have been funny if he didn't watch her so intently. If that direct eye contact didn't make her entire body simply *ignite*.

Under that stuffy exterior, Zach was proving to be a very, *very* dangerous variable in this whole mess. Because along with stalkers she didn't know what to do with, murder that scared her to her bones, and guilt that nearly ate her alive, she was still herself. Daisy Delaney. Lucy Cooper.

And she'd never been very good at pulling her hand out of the fire.

ZACH NEEDED MORE SLEEP. Clearly, a lack of it was the cause of his current lack of control.

Not that he'd done anything aside from watch her steal a scoop of his ice cream. And open her mouth around the spoon. And swallow the bite.

Then nearly spontaneously combust.

He looked down at his ice cream and tried to remember anything about what they were talking about. Anything that wasn't her mouth, or the way she'd leaned against him in the bedroom earlier.

He should cut himself a little slack. He was only human after all, and she was beautiful and engaging. She had that *thing* that made people want to watch her, get wrapped up in her orbit.

Maybe he'd like to be immune, but he was hardly a failure just because he wasn't.

But the one and only time he'd let his emotions get the best of him people had almost died. People he cared about. People he loved.

He couldn't—wouldn't—make that mistake again. No matter how tempting Daisy Delaney proved herself to be.

All his paperwork was in his room, as was his laptop. He had no shields to wield against her, and he had to think of this as its own version of war, even if it was only a war within himself.

"You could reach out and say you're willing to do a few shows," he said. He might not have his papers, but that didn't mean they couldn't talk through some options. When in doubt, focus on the task at hand. When tempted beyond reason, focus on what needed to be done.

"That'd go through my agent—the actual booking."

"Does your agent know you're here?"

"No. Not unless Stacy told him. I doubt

she would have. She would have just told him I'm unavailable."

Maybe. The problem was, you never really knew what people told other people, and who those other people knew. There were so many fraying threads and he felt frayed himself. By her, by all this close proximity and by this damn dogged frustration that the case wasn't as simple as he might have thought.

"What about Jordan?"

She slumped, toying with her spoon. It amazed him the way she'd been mostly blamed and decimated in the press for being the instigator, the uncaring party, while Jordan poured his brokenhearted soul into his next album.

But every time Zach mentioned her ex-husband, she had a visceral reaction—in ways she didn't with other topics.

It twisted something inside him he refused to investigate, because emotions had to stay out of this. No more guitars. No more going into her room if she was having a nightmare. No more...

She took another bite of his ice cream.

Zach kept his gaze on his bowl. No more ice cream sharing, that was for sure.

"What *about* Jordan?" she asked, giving up on his ice cream and her own frozen yogurt.

"Would anyone have told him where you are? Does he have any connections to your manager or your agent?"

"He got a new agent when we got divorced. We never shared managers, though I guess Stacy was friends with Doug. In the way two people who sometimes have to work together are friends. She knows… Look, she was there through the divorce. She wouldn't give Jordan any information, and I don't think my agent is a fan of Jordan's after the way he was treated."

*Or maybe he's not a fan of yours.* Zach made a mental note to look deeper into the agent. "I don't really understand the ins and outs of your…what would you call it, staff?"

"Team," she replied emphatically.

"Let's go over the hierarchy there."

She shook her head. "I think I'd rather go back to bed and take my chances with nightmares."

"That's fine."

She eyed him. "It's fine, but be prepared to do it in the morning?"

Zach shrugged. "I have to dig, Daisy."

"No, you actually don't. You just have to keep me alive."

It was true. He hadn't been hired to investigate. He'd been hired to protect. But that didn't mean he couldn't or wouldn't do both.

He needed her cooperation, though, which meant he had to go about getting the information a little more…strategically.

"You're right," he said, doing his best to sound like he agreed with her. "I don't have to poke into this or you. It's not my job." He stood, taking both bowls and walking them to the sink. "I'll butt out."

He turned, ready to head to his room. If temper flared a little unsteadily inside him, he snuffed it out. Emotions weren't his job, either.

Not investigating wasn't an option for him. But if she didn't want him digging into it, he'd do it without her.

She stood and stepped very deliberately into his path to his door. She cocked her head, studying him in a way that reminded him of being back in the FBI Academy—constantly being sized up for his effectiveness and usefulness.

He hadn't minded it then. He'd been full of the utter certainty that he belonged there, and that he was more than fit to be an agent.

Now, here, it scraped along his skin, unearthing too many insecurities he'd much rather pretend didn't exist.

"You did one hell of a job undercover, didn't you?" she murmured.

He was surprised at the change in topic,

but he didn't let any of his unaffected poise loosen. "I suppose."

"The problem now is that you aren't undercover, so when you put on the act it doesn't add up."

"I don't follow."

"You don't care if investigating isn't your job. You're going to do it anyway. You don't let things go, and one way or another, you'll keep poking at me. There's something under this…" She waved her fingers in front of his face. "I'd say I don't understand it, but I do. I may not have grown up with my brother, but I recognize that cop thing—truth and justice above all else."

"So I remind you of your brother," he said flatly.

Her mouth curved, slowly, and with way too much enjoyment. The move so slow and fluid and mesmerizing he watched it the entire time—from mouth quirk to full-on sultry smile.

"No, I can't say you do, Zach."

He wanted to shift, to clear his throat, to do *anything* that might loosen all this tightening inside him. But it would be a giveaway.

*Would it matter if you gave it away to her? She isn't your enemy.*

"But what I will say is that if it wasn't for

my brother, I wouldn't believe in the existence of good men with an inner sense of right and wrong and a deep-seated need to protect."

He held still. He met her gaze with all the blankness he'd honed in his time undercover. You made eye contact, but you didn't fall into it. You didn't get conned into believing you could act so well that someone saw what you wanted them to see.

So you gave nothing. You counted eyelashes or recited the Gettysburg Address. You didn't think over your plan, and you didn't give in to trying to analyze their thoughts or feelings—because thoughts and feelings couldn't be analyzed or predicted. They couldn't be patterned out.

Which, unfortunately for Daisy, was why he thought this whole thing was *personal*. Someone who wanted to hurt her for something more than her music or her reputation.

"So you can keep poking at me, and I'll keep poking back, but that doesn't mean I don't understand what you're trying to do. It doesn't mean I don't want you to do it. It means I'm frustrated and you're an easy target. All that rational, factual thought is the rock I can toss my irrational emotion against. And isn't that nice?" She patted his chest.

"Maybe we'll even get to the point where we enjoy all the…poking."

He might have risen to the bait. Laughed or coughed or fidgeted at her overt sexual innuendo, but he knew that no matter how smart or worried she was, she was hoping whoever was terrorizing her was a random stranger and his investigation was pointless.

He couldn't let her think that by getting distracted over her purposeful baiting. Because it didn't fit, in Zach's mind. Whoever was doing this *knew* her, and it was very possible Daisy trusted them.

He didn't have to tell her that. He didn't have to poke at her—in any way, shape or form—though he might have wanted to rest his hand over hers…*just* to offer a little comfort.

Instead, he held still. Unearthly still. He kept her gaze, until that easy, flirtatious grin of hers faded.

"Your safety is my primary concern. However, it isn't my job or my aim to cause you undue emotional distress. Therefore, if my method of questioning is problematic, I can easily engage in other avenues of investigation that don't require any…" He desperately wanted to say *poking*. Wanted to smile and make a joke and ease all of that sudden tension out of her.

But maybe it would be better for everyone if there was a little tension that kept them from being too friendly.

"That don't require any avenues of questioning that might feel problematic on either of our ends."

She blinked. "Primary concern," she echoed. "Emotional distress." She shook her head and took a few steps back. The look she gave him was one of suspicion.

Since it wasn't his job to have her *trust* him, such a look couldn't bother him at all.

At all.

"Yeah, I bet you were a *hell* of an undercover agent, Zach," she muttered, but she was gathering herself. She was sharpening all those tools she so effectively used against him—an insightfulness, a confidence that she lashed against him like a weapon. "But news flash. You aren't anymore. Keeping me safe, investigating this thing, you can be regular old Zach Simmons, and it'll be more than enough."

*How would that ever be enough?*

But he couldn't say that to anyone, could he? So he merely nodded. "Noted."

Then, with absolutely no warning, she

stepped forward again. She reached out and touched his face—a gentle caress one might bestow upon a loved one. She held his gaze with a softness he couldn't possibly understand.

Then she did the most incomprehensible thing he had ever in his entire life witnessed or been on the receiving end of.

She lifted onto her toes and pressed her mouth to his.

# *Chapter Seven*

It was wrong. Daisy had been well aware of that when she'd done it. Maybe she'd even done it because it was wrong.

But he'd laid down a challenge—whether he'd known it or not. He'd tried to turn off his personality, his entire essence. He'd tried to use the robot on her and that had only spurred her on to try to short-circuit the robot.

She would never again be told she didn't really mean anything, that she could be easily moved aside and closed off in a room without a second thought. No. Not for a man she'd been married to and not for a man who'd been tasked to keep her safe.

She would show *him*. She would get to him. And what better way to do that than to use her mouth?

His initial stiffness was shock, obviously, but when she didn't move away, changing the angle of the kiss instead, something shuddered through him.

Or maybe something broke inside him. *She'd* broken something inside him, because he didn't just return the kiss—he started one of his own.

Not a challenge or some kind of attempt at one-upmanship. This was...just a kiss, except *just* didn't fit.

It was real. It was Zach. As if a few days under the same roof could make you feel things for one another. But his mouth crushed against hers like they were longtime lovers, used to the act of kissing enough to have it practiced, but not so much that it didn't *melt*. A warmth that soaked into her bloodstream like alcohol, and a sudden weakness she knew she'd regret at some point.

But there was nothing to regret now with Zach's mouth on hers, his arms drawing her closer so that she was pressed against all that muscle and restraint.

Except there was nothing *restrained* about how he kissed her. It wasn't the explosion of lust she might have expected or understood. It was deeper, stronger. The kind of thing that didn't rock you for a moment, but forever. A kiss she'd remember *forever*.

Maybe because that thought horrified her

enough to startle, Zach broke the kiss. He pulled his mouth from hers and nudged her back and away from him. Her knees might have been weak, but she saw a flicker of *something* in his gaze. Some kind of complicated emotion that disappeared before she could get a handle on what he might be feeling.

He fixed her with a gaze, and spoke with utter certainty. "This will never happen again."

She absolutely *hated* the way he said *never*, as if he were God himself and got to decree the way the world worked, the way *she* worked. So she smiled, all razor-edged sweetness. "Zach, don't you know better than to challenge me by now?"

"Do you want to *die*?" he asked with such a bald-faced certainty her insides turned to ice. Immediately.

"I don't know how a kiss is going to kill me," she managed, though she sounded shaken. She *was* shaken. Even with the ice of fear shifting everything inside her, her limbs felt like jelly.

She could still feel Zach's mouth on hers. He'd wanted her, or was it all another act? A mask?

No, he might be blank now but there was a kind of anger radiating off him. One she didn't understand because it didn't show up in any of the ways anger usually did. No yelling, no fisted hands, no threats or furious gazes. Not even the condescending sigh Jordan had perfected during their short marriage.

"You are in a dangerous situation," Zach said, and his robot voice was back but it frayed along the edges. "Potentially a life-or-death situation, and you're adding..." He sucked in a breath and then slowly let it out. His next words were no more inflected, but they were softer. "Listen to me, as someone who's been in a few life-or-death situations myself. The only thing that happens when you tangle emotion into dangerous situations is catastrophe."

"It was just a kiss," she managed, wincing at how petulant she sounded.

"It was a complication. One you can't afford."

That stoked some of her irritation back to high. She lifted her chin. "Don't presume to tell me what I can afford."

"Are you always so damn difficult?" he demanded, the slightest hint of a snap to his tone.

"If you have to ask that, you haven't been paying attention."

He rolled his eyes, and she had no doubt she was about to be dismissed. Part of her wanted to throw a fit, make herself into more of a nuisance, but her surroundings were too much of a reminder of where her fits and anger and *feelings* had gotten her.

A failed marriage *everyone* got to have a say about. Isolation and loneliness that went deep because so many people were willing to believe the worst about her and think she deserved whatever she got.

Kissing Zach had been a mistake. She felt suddenly sick to her stomach at how much of one. Thoughtless reaction, plain and simple. When would she ever learn?

*Mr. Control kissed you, too.*

And since when did someone else's culpability matter to her end result?

His phone chimed in his pocket and he pulled it out, clicking a few things. His expression never changed.

But it was something like four in the morning. Who would be contacting him at four in the morning? Only someone with bad news, and since she was his current bad news...

"What is it? Is someone hurt? Is Vaughn—"

He shook his head sharply. "My cousin's wife had her baby."

Zach didn't exactly strike her as the type to receive middle of the night texts about a cousin's baby. "Don't lie to me about—"

He held out the phone and on the screen there

was a picture of a red-faced baby wrapped in pink. Underneath the picture the text read:

Amelia Delaney Carson, 6 lbs 11 oz, 20 inches. Batten down the hatches.

It was *odd* that a pang could wallop her out of nowhere, when she'd convinced herself that she wasn't even sure she ever wanted babies. That she and Jordan had come to the conclusion they wouldn't rush bringing *children* into the world when they had careers to build.

But her career had already been built, and what she hadn't admitted to herself was that she'd been hoping marriage would be a transition of sorts.

What she'd really wanted out of marrying Jordan had been a home. Full of music and joy and no tours or constant travel. Stability. She'd dreamed of a peaceful life. Not one devoid of performing, of being *Daisy Delaney*, but one where she got to choose when and where to play the role.

Daisy *was* her, and she loved that persona. But it had been her whole childhood and adolescence, and the older she got the more she felt like she'd earned a little time for Lucy Cooper.

Why she thought she'd be able to build that

with Jordan, in that distant future he always talked about, was beyond her.

She handed the phone back to Zach. "Cute," she managed to offer. "I like the middle name."

He made an odd face. "It's the mother's last name," he offered, studying her warily.

"A Wyoming Delaney?"

He very nearly *winced*, which she couldn't quite figure though she decided to enjoy his discomfort anyhow.

"Do you know... Wyoming Delaneys?" he asked, failing at the odd casual tone he was clearly trying to maintain. "I mean, Daisy Delaney is a stage name, though."

He seemed a little too desperate to believe it was true. "Yes and no. Why does that weird you out? Worried we're related or something?"

"Carsons and Delaneys aren't related."

"I thought you were a Simmons."

He shook his head. "Anyway. We should try to get some sleep. We'll come up with some things to tell your manager and see if we can't get a lead."

She studied him. There was something weird about his discomfort over the shared name. Since she was more than a little irritated with him, she wanted to poke at it. "My legal name might be Cooper, but my stage name was my grandmother's name before she got married. Daisy Delaney. She was born in some little town in Wyoming. Something with a B? I'd have to text Vaughn. He'd remember. Oh, wait, it was Bent. That's why Daddy always used to wear his hell bound and whiskey *bent* shirt."

"Jesus," Zach muttered, looking so downright horrified she nearly laughed.

"What?"

"Nothing," he said far too quickly.

"Are we close to there?"

"Kind of. Anyway. Bed."

"Maybe I'm related to your cousin's wife. Wouldn't that be a trip?"

"Yeah, a real trip. Goodnight, Daisy."

ZACH WAS TIRED of women. Particularly opinionated ones. Pretty ones. Infuriating ones.

He really didn't need his sister to add to it, but here she was, trying to tell him what to do.

"You have to come," she said, her tone something closer to a demand than he was used to hearing from her. Still, it seemed every day Hilly got a little more confident, a little more situated to life outside the isolated cabin she'd been raised in.

He stood on the dilapidated porch of the

building that usually gave him such satisfaction. After last night, not much did.

"I'm in the middle of a job. I can't just leave Daisy here locked up."

"You could bring her with you."

"Yes, that's genius. She has some kind of stalker snooping around Bent, so why don't I bring her to the hospital and potentially endanger every member of our family." *And hers, apparently.* Because Daisy Delaney's grandmother was from Bent, Wyoming.

He didn't believe in all the metaphysical nonsense spouted by his cousins—that the old Carson and Delaney feud had morphed into Carson and Delaney unions that were meant to be.

He didn't believe in meant-to-be.

"Are you okay?" Hilly asked.

The fact she even suspected he wasn't caused him to straighten, to remind himself he didn't have *time* for stupid worries over stupid nonsense.

"Of course I am. But this job is important. And we haven't found any solid leads. I can't leave her here, and I can't risk taking her somewhere else."

"She can't possibly still want to be cooped up in there."

"Hilly."

"I know. I know. Safety. Precautions. But…" She looked up at the dilapidated building. "How long can you feasibly keep her in this place? It's going to start to feel like a prison."

"Better a prison than a coffin, Hilly."

"Why do you have to be so *practical*?" she muttered.

"I believe it's in the job description."

"But your life isn't a job description, Zach. And neither is Daisy's."

Zach didn't know what other string of words would get her to stop this incessant merry-go-round. The flash of something far off in the distance put him on instant alert— enough so he no longer cared about words. Only getting her away.

"We're going to walk to your car. Once you're inside, I want you to call…" He racked his brain for someone who'd be able to help. Cam needed to watch the other guy. Most of his family was at the hospital with Laurel and Grady. Getting the cops involved would be tricky.

"What is it?" Hilly asked, her voice perfectly even, her expression still mildly bemused. But she understood.

He took her by the arm and they strolled back to her car. "Someone's out there."

He needed to make it look like he wasn't

living here. He needed to lead the man somewhere else. And somehow, he had to get in contact with Daisy so she knew to stay the hell put.

"I couldn't have been followed. Cam's sitting on the guy." Hilly smiled brightly up at him as if he'd just said something hilarious.

"Well, then we have a second guy."

"All right. I'll call Cam and head his way. We'll come up with something. Don't worry about me. Keep Daisy safe."

"I don't want him following you."

"You can't want him staying here."

It was too close. Too dangerous. Unless he played all his cards right. "Go. Call Cam."

For the first time her cheerful, just-talking-to-my-brother facade faded. "I don't trust that tone, Zach."

"Trust the man who used to be the FBI agent, Hilly."

She hesitated, which cut like a knife even though she had every reason to doubt him. Hadn't Cam almost died because Zach had been too concerned about his brother's welfare to take care of business?

"I don't want you doing something on your own."

"I won't be on my own. I'll have you calling Cam for backup. But I need you to go on the chance he does follow you." Zach was counting on the former, but if it was the latter…

Well, he had a plan for that, too.

Eliminate the threat.

"Drive to Cam. Okay?"

"All right. Only because I can't think of a better plan. Do not do anything on your own, do you hear me?"

"I hear you."

She sighed disgustedly, presumably because she knew *I hear you* didn't mean he agreed to anything she'd said.

She reached out and took his hand, giving it a squeeze. She forced a smile for the sake of whoever might be watching them. "Just be careful. Because if you get hurt, I will have to end you." Her smile was a little more genuine at the end, and she turned and got in her car.

Zach couldn't spare a glance for the house, for Daisy. He stood exactly where he was and watched Hilly's car disappear.

Whoever was out there didn't follow.

Zach didn't head back into the house, and he didn't check on his sidearm or his phone, though he wanted to grab for both.

He didn't know who or what was out there. Someone could be watching, it could be a vehicle left behind as someone approached town on foot. It could be his eyes playing tricks on him, but the back of his neck prickled with foreboding.

Which meant taking every precaution necessary.

He walked down the dusty side of the road as if he didn't have a care in the world. He even forced himself to whistle. He turned down the alley, keeping up the act of unhurried unflappability.

Once he was around the corner, he sprang into action. He'd been keeping his car hidden since that first day, just so no one happened upon it. He popped open the hidden keypad on the garage hidden in the building. He entered his code and moved as quickly as he could, watching for anyone who might pop into view. There was the possibility whoever had been watching was trying to break in the house, but that would take time.

He'd use it.

He drove the car out and closed up the hidden garage. When he pulled out of the alley, there was no sign of anyone trying to get into the house. So he took the opposite way out of his town at a slow pace.

He caught the flash again. This time he could tell it was a small compact car half hidden behind one of the far buildings in town. He couldn't make out the license plate—number or state—only the black fender glinting in the sun.

He kept his breathing in check and drove on, remaining slow and unhurried and looking around, pretending to smile as he enjoyed the beautiful Wyoming landscape.

When the car didn't follow after several minutes, he swore.

They suspected someone besides him was in town, and that was absolutely no good. So he swerved off the road and ditched the car. Since he wasn't being followed, he didn't worry about hiding it. Time was more important.

He ran back the way he'd driven, darting behind buildings on the opposite side of the car and mostly tried to keep out of sight of the car.

He stopped for a second on the opposite side of the road as the house Daisy was in. He stilled and listened.

No motor running, so they wouldn't have a head start on him. But he didn't like their proximity to Daisy. Because he couldn't even be sure someone was in the car. Whoever was watching could have gotten out to start snooping around the house.

He wished he knew how long they'd been there and that he could be sure the car had followed Hilly. Because if they hadn't followed Hilly, they had more information than Zach liked to consider.

Either way, Daisy had a leak and now she was in the direct line of fire.

Which meant Zach had to move. And fast.

# Chapter Eight

Daisy impatiently tapped her fingers against the countertop. Where the hell was Zach? It wasn't like him to stay holed up in his room with the door closed, though she supposed he might have had a break in the case or was making phone calls he didn't want her to hear.

Since *she'd* been holed up in her room strumming on the guitar he'd gifted her, it was more than possible he'd left. She couldn't fathom him doing that without telling her, no matter how irritated he was about the kiss.

She smiled to herself. Oh, the moments after hadn't been any fun, but the in-the-moment had been something she'd willingly relive over and over again.

It was the first time in a while where she'd felt…normal. Like Lucy Cooper, or even the Daisy Delaney from years ago when she hadn't had anything normal outside the music. There had been a simplicity in that time.

Of course, there was nothing simple about being either version of herself now, and certainly nothing simple about the aftermath of kissing Zach.

Still, she gave herself permission, here alone, to enjoy the memory of something she could pretend was simple.

The slight creaking sound brought Daisy out of the memory. She tried to shake away the wiggle of alarm. It was an old house—no matter what improvements Zach had made—of course it creaked.

But in the silence that ensued after, her heart beat harder until it became such a loud thud she knew she wouldn't hear the sound again even if it came from one of the walls.

She looked around, trying to remind herself she was safe. Locked and hidden away.

*But someone knows you're nearby.*

She marched over to Zach's door. She wouldn't tell him about the noise. She'd just insist he give her some information. Maybe she'd come on to him. Whatever it took so that he was around and making her feel safe.

She knocked. Harder than she should have.

He didn't answer.

Alarm went from a wiggle to a flop. She grabbed the knob and tried to turn it.

Locked.

The wiggles and flops turned into chains that restricted her breathing. "Zach," she croaked. She cursed herself for the nerves, the fear, the total ineffectuality of her voice. She breathed in and out, tried to use some of her old tricks for the occasional bout of stage fright.

"Zach," she repeated, louder this time but more firm. Surely, he'd hear it through the door.

Nothing happened.

She wouldn't panic. Couldn't. She pounded against the door for a while, but then she heard something else—a creak, a moan. Something definitely from the outside. Which meant if there was someone other than Zach outside, they could definitely hear the banging.

But he had to be in there. He was probably trying to teach her a lesson or something. Scare her so she'd stop hitting on him. Yes, that had to be what this was.

Well, wouldn't he be sorry? She marched to the kitchen, ignoring the way her hands shook and her heart beat a painful, panicked cadence. She grabbed a butter knife and marched back to the door and got to work.

It took longer than she would have preferred as she had to wiggle the knife in the slot, then between the door and the frame. She was shaking at this point. Where *was* he? She thought for sure he'd pop out if she started trying to break into his room. Surely, he'd only locked it to keep her out.

The door finally gave and she swung it open. "Aha!" she yelled, pointing the knife into the room.

But it was empty. She moved around, searching every corner and under the bed, even the closet.

No one. Not a soul.

"Oh, God. God. Zach, if this is some kind of joke or test, I'm over it."

But he didn't appear, and those *noises* kept coming from outside this hellhole disguised as a safe place.

Panic bubbled through her, paralyzing her limbs and squeezing her throat. Her heart beat too hard in her ears and she desperately wanted to scream.

But she'd been through worse than being left alone. Seeing Tom dead was the worst. No one had a right to make it worse than that.

Then something rustled in the closet. Something big. But she'd just been in that closet. How could—

A figure stepped out and she screamed before her brain could accept that it was Zach *miraculously* showing up out of nowhere.

"How did you do that?" she whispered. He wasn't *magic*. There had to be an explanation.

"Tunnel. Shoes."

"Tunnel shoes? What does that—"

"Get some damn shoes, Daisy. Purse if it's handy. Ten seconds." Without further explanation he strode out of the room and into the kitchen. She scurried after him but stopped short when he pulled two guns out of the top cabinet above the refrigerator while she only stared.

Until he gave her a sharp look.

"Move," he ordered, snapping her out of her shock.

She had to move. Questions were clearly for later when he wasn't grabbing extra guns. She hurried into her room, shoved her feet into tennis shoes and looked around for her purse. Ten seconds. She had way less than ten seconds now and she was not the neatest person on the planet.

But she caught a glimpse of the strap under her duffel bag and lunged for it, tugged it from the haphazardly spilled-out bag and ran back to Zach. He held a laptop across one arm while he typed with the other, a huge backpack strapped over his back.

When she peered over his shoulder at the screen of the laptop—which had been full of pictures of the ghost town they were in—he snapped it shut. "The front is the best option. Follow me. *Stick* to me. Do whatever I say without question and everything will be fine. If something happens to me, no matter what, you run. You understand me?"

"Zach. I don't understand *anything*."

"We'll figure it out when we're safe." He took her by the hand and pulled her to the door.

Even as a million questions assaulted her, she understood Zach Simmons was not a man to overreact. If he wanted them to run, she'd run.

He pulled her out into the first room that looked as dilapidated as the outside. "Lock the locks," he said, handing her a key chain with three keys on it. They weren't labeled, but she didn't ask which one was for which—she just kept trying till she had all three locks locked.

He was peering at something through the wall. "See that picture frame on the ground?"

She looked down. There was an old, battered picture frame with a ripped piece of paper inside. "Uh, yeah."

"Hang it up on that rusty nail."

She did so, and blinked as it perfectly hid the key holes from view.

"Now, come hold my hand again."

She wanted to make a joke about hitting on her, but the words stuck in her throat. They were running, and that couldn't be good.

So she slid her hand into his and let him pull her along. He slid out the door, and she followed suit. He didn't lock this door, instead left a rusty-looking padlock hanging off the handle.

His gaze swept everywhere, and then he gave her hand a squeeze. "Now we run. I'm not going to be able to hold your hand without whacking you with the bag, so you'll just have to follow me. If you can't keep up—"

"I'll keep up." No matter what.

He nodded firmly. "Good. All right. Let's go."

He moved across the dusty road, and it was only then she realized he held the closed laptop in one hand and a gun in another. Still, she followed him, behind one building, and then through the alley between two even worse-off ones. Caved-in roofs, fire-scorched walls.

He reached the small ramshackle building at the end of the road and handed off his laptop to her while hanging on to his gun. With his free hand, he reached through a jagged break in the glass window of the back door, fiddling around until the door popped open.

He slowly pulled his arm out, and then

opened the door just as slowly. It took her a minute to realize he was trying to mitigate the squeaking noise that echoed through the air as he opened it. When the opening was big enough, he gestured her inside.

Trying not to balk at the dark, or the spiderwebs, she stepped into the dank, smelly interior. Zach followed suit, pulling the door closed behind him before fishing a flashlight out of his pack.

He led her farther inside and she kept waiting for the nice part—the part that had been redone inside all the dilapidation.

But this one had no new pretty interior. No working kitchen. It was abandoned and untouched for years. "We're going to stay... here?"

Zach had put his pack on the floor and took his laptop back without a word. She was sure he wasn't paying any attention to her at all as he worked furiously.

When he finally spoke, she fairly jumped with adrenaline.

"*You're* going to stay here. I'm going to figure out what the hell is going on. You know how to shoot a gun?"

She blinked at the weapon he held out to her. Thanks to her brother, she'd had a few shooting lessons. She was even somewhat familiar with the kind Zach held out to her.

She nodded, and he handed the gun over.

"Anyone comes in here that isn't me or Cam, or doesn't say the code word *feud*, you shoot. Understood?"

She swallowed, and managed another nod.

With that, he got to his feet, strapped multiple guns to his person and strode for the door.

ZACH SLID OUT of the building, making sure no one was around to see him. It was painful to leave Daisy wide-eyed, scared and alone, but he couldn't hole up with her and hope the guys went away.

He'd learned, over and over again, that waiting in safety often caused more problems than it solved. Sometimes you had to act to keep people safe.

He hurried behind the buildings, keeping his body out of sight from as many angles as possible.

From what he'd been able to tell with his video surveillance, there were two men. One who'd been poking around the house, and the one who'd stayed in the car—presumably ready to drive off.

It turned his stomach to think he was ready

to drive off with Daisy. Even more so that *two* men were here.

It had to be the manager leaking information to someone, whether maliciously or with an accidental slip to someone. He didn't have time to figure out the pattern, though. He had to stop those men before they had a chance to hurt Daisy.

He moved into a position where he knew he'd be able to see the driver of the car with minimal chance of being detected. He angled his body and his head, and managed to make out the car.

The driver was no longer in it, so Zach moved forward—until he saw both of them standing in front of the car, discussing something.

They had their backs to him, so descriptions would be hard, but it wouldn't matter. These weren't the masterminds trying to get to Daisy. Everything about them screamed hired muscle.

Which, again, in Zach's mind meant not a crazed fan, but someone with a personal connection. And someone with money.

Like Jordan Jones.

And if it *was* Jordan, he'd have endless funds to keep sending people just like this.

Zach moved back behind the building. Tak-

ing them out was only a temporary solution.
More would come in their place. But if he
could question them, he might be able to glean
enough information to make the connection.

The only question was how to immobilize
the threat of two men with guns who wanted
the woman he was trying to protect.

He needed them to separate, and even then
it would be risky. But it would be a risk he'd
have to take. He examined the building he was
hiding in. He needed somewhere he could isolate one man, without getting trapped by both.

He needed to get one headed in the other direction. He pulled the phone out of his pocket
and pulled up the app he used to control security in the safe house. He poked around until
he came up with an idea.

Have the back door alarm on the house go
off. Once they started heading over, he'd make
enough noise they'd feel like one of them had
to come his way.

It took a few minutes—first the men headed
toward the siren, alert and with hands on their
weapons. Zach kicked at a board next to him,
the hard crack of impact then splitting wood
loud enough to hopefully get one's attention.

He couldn't watch for their approach. Instead, he had to stay hidden and hope he was
about to fight only one man.

He saw the gun first and immediately moved. He kicked the gun out of the man's hand. The man leaped forward, but Zach had better vision and grabbed him from behind. Zach managed to get an arm around the other man's throat. Zach was taller, though the man was thicker.

"Who are you?" Zach demanded in a whisper as the man struggled against him.

The man didn't answer, and no one came to his rescue. Elsewhere, the alarm continued to beep, which was a good sound cover for the fight Zach was about to have here.

"Who sent you?" Zach asked, tightening his grip and dodging the man's attempt at backward blows.

The response was only a raspy laugh as he twisted and nearly got free before Zach strengthened the choke hold.

They grappled, but Zach kept the choke hold. He asked a few more questions, knowing he wouldn't get an answer but hoping he might get *something* that would ID the man or give him a hint.

Over the sound of his alarm, he heard something else. Something just as shrill. Sirens in the distance. It was unlikely to be coincidence that sirens were closing in on the empty ghost town. Cam and Hilly must have decided to call the cops. Hell. Zach sure hoped they'd sent more than one because he had no doubt that the other guy was now on his way back.

"You think the cops will help you? Or her, for that matter?" the man rasped.

"Guess we'll find out." Zach managed to jerk one of the man's arms behind his back, but it left him open to an elbow to the gut. His grip loosened just enough to have the man slip out of his grasp.

The man tried to take off on a run, but Zach lunged, tackling him to the ground. They tussled, landing blows. The other man was bigger but Zach figured he could hold his own until the cop car actually got here.

The next blow rattled his cage pretty good, so much so that he thought he heard a dog bark and growl.

But then there really was a dog, growling and leaping. Zach had a moment of fear before he recognized the dog, and it jumped at his attacker. The man screamed, and Zach managed to wrangle himself free of his grasp.

A cop appeared, gun held and trained on the man on the ground—the man who was clearly scared to death as the dog growled and snapped right next to his face.

"Free. Sit," Hilly's voice called.

The dog stopped growling, planted its butt

on the ground and wagged its tail before turning his head toward Zach.

"Thanks for the assist." He gave the dog a rubdown, wincing only a little as his face throbbed. He glanced up as Hilly, who'd given her dog the command, came running. He was a little surprised when she kneeled next to him instead of her dog, Free.

"You're bleeding." She ran her hands over him as if checking for breaks or injuries, but he held her off.

"It's just a split lip. Please tell me Cam is here and you didn't try to white knight this yourself."

"It wasn't just me. I had Free. Plus the cops."

Zach swore, but he couldn't muster up much heat behind it. "I've got to get to Daisy." He glanced at the Bent County Sheriff's Deputy who was handcuffing the man who'd attacked him. Deputy Keenland efficiently did the job and read the man his rights.

"There's another one," Zach offered.

"We've already got him," the cop replied.

"I want to talk to them."

Keenland gave him a raised eyebrow. "We'll be transporting them to the station, where *we'll* question them. We'll take your report, as well."

He didn't have time for this. He glanced at Hilly. He didn't even have to ask. She nodded.

"Far building on this side," he said quietly so Keenland, busy pulling the arrested man to his feet, wouldn't hear.

He'd have to entrust Daisy to Hilly while he took care of this. It bugged him, but it had to be done. He pulled out his phone and turned off the security so Hilly could get into his apps, and then handed her his phone and his keys to the building.

"Be careful." They all needed to be a hell of a lot more careful.

# Chapter Nine

Back in the fake nice house inside an outside dilapidated old house, Daisy couldn't find any of the calm or resignation she'd had in the days leading up to this.

Someone had found her here. Maybe they hadn't gotten to her, but they'd tried. In this place that was supposed to be a secret from everyone.

Which meant someone she loved and trusted was either out to hurt her, or close enough to someone who did to slip the information to them.

God, her head hurt. Almost as much as her heart as she went back over so many interactions.

Could Jaime be the bad link? She didn't know him that well, even if he was Vaughn's brother-in-law. He could have told anyone, couldn't he? But Zach trusted him. Surely, Zach would know…

Except Zach wanted her to believe Stacy was responsible. Could her manager harbor some secret hatred of her? Was it as simple, and heartbreaking, as that?

Or was it deeper, messier, more complicated?

Worse than the riot of emotions and fear and questions pulsing inside her, Cam and Hilly were being obnoxiously and carefully tight-lipped about what exactly had gone down after Zach had left her in the abandoned house.

Only that he'd be back soon to explain everything. But time kept ticking by as she sat at the table, watching Cam and Hilly.

Which was actually the worst part of all. Hilly and Cam moved around the kitchen and common area acting like the perfect unit. A team. A partnership.

She felt so completely alone. The separation of the past few years echoing inside her like she'd been emptied out—of love and companionship and hope. There was only fear left.

She rested her forehead on the table and did everything she could to keep from crying. No one was going to see her cry. Nope. She would brazen through this like she'd brazened through everything else in her life.

Maybe she was tired. Maybe she wanted *normal* for a little bit. Maybe she wanted a little house in the country and a nice man she could trust to build a family with.

And maybe Daisy Delaney and Lucy Cooper weren't made for those things.

Her phone chimed and she nearly fell over lunging for it on the table. Surely, it would have to be Zach. Everyone else had stopped calling and texting and surely—

She stared at the text message from Jordan. The first sentence made her uneasy, so she clicked it to read the whole thing.

I just heard you're out of town for a few days. Someone told me it might be rehab. I really hope you get the help you need. Peace to you.

Peace. Peace? Anger surged through her, and while some of it was prompted by all the fear and things out of her control right now, most of it was prompted by that *ridiculous* send-off.

Peace to you.

*Peace.*

She'd like to give him some peace. Right up his—

"Is everything okay?" Hilly asked gently, but with concern.

Daisy smiled up at Hilly, though she knew

it came out too sharp when Hilly took a step back. "Yes. Just a text from an annoying…acquaintance. Apparently, the rumor is I'm in rehab." She wanted to bash the phone into little bits. "How do I respond to a text like that?"

"You don't," Cam said in a voice that reminded Daisy of Zach.

Where *was* he?

"You'll have to excuse me if I don't want the world thinking I'm in rehab. My reputation is in enough tatters."

"But if people think you're in rehab, they won't think you're *here*," Cam replied reasonably. Apparently, whatever trouble had happened had cured him of his slight starstruck nature. Or he was just getting used to her.

Daisy couldn't say she cared for it. "Whoever is after me already knows I'm here."

"But the fewer people who know, the fewer people your stalker can use to get to you."

It was so reasonable, really unarguable, and now she wanted to bash her phone against Cam. She was tired of being reasonable in all these impossible situations. She wanted to act out. She wanted to *fight*.

She wanted to tell Jordan to go jump off a cliff. Or write a song about lighting all his prized possessions on fire.

One by one.

But Cam was right and Daisy's only choice was sitting here, not responding, not reacting. Just waiting for someone to succeed in hurting her.

"Did Zach okay the cell phone use?" Cam asked, his attempt at casual almost fooling her into thinking it was a generic question.

"Yes, thank you very much. He did something to my phone to block traces or something. But he wanted me to be able to email my agent from my phone and a few other things. I don't know. Techie stuff. But it's perfectly Zach-approved." Because everything in her life now suddenly was Zach-approved.

Except herself. She could still rile him up to the best of her ability. Assuming he came back and didn't abandon her here.

She closed her eyes, nearly giving in to tears again. Oh, God. That was what she was *really* afraid of. Not that someone had found her, but now that they had, Zach would leave her.

Hilly pushed a mug and plate at her.

"Drink some tea. And eat some cookies."

"You Simmonses and your ungodly sugar addiction." An unexpected lump formed in her throat. "Where *is* he?" she asked, hating that the emotion leaked out in her scratchy voice.

Hilly patted her hand. "He's safe, and he'll be back soon."

She didn't need him to come back. She didn't *need* Zach Simmons. At *all*. He was a bodyguard, more or less.

But God, she wanted him here pushing cookies on her, telling her what the next step would be, and reassuring her he'd take care of everything.

"FIVE MINUTES."

The deputy didn't move, didn't even spare him another condescending look. "We've taken your statement, Mr. Simmons. You're free to leave."

"I need five minutes. Hell, I'll settle for two questions."

"Simmons."

Zach turned around and sighed. Detective Thomas Hart stood, plain-clothed, in the doorway, and Zach knew he was officially done.

He followed Hart out of the building and into the parking lot. It was dark now, and Zach wasn't all that sure he knew how much time had passed. But he hadn't gotten what he wanted yet.

"There has to be something you can tell me."

"There isn't. Sincerely. He's not giving us answers."

"I want a name, Hart. A last known address."

Hart turned, crossed his arms over his

chest. "You won't get one. Stop harassing the deputies. Go home. Deal with whatever business you've got going down on your own."

"I can hack into your system in five seconds flat," Zach returned disgustedly.

Hart held up a finger. "First, I didn't hear you say that. Second, be my guest. Because I can't give you that information. Zach, you know as well as I do, whatever they're after—however it connects to your mysterious business—these guys are hired muscle. They're not going to tell you or me anything you really need to know."

"But you'll investigate who's paying them."

"If it's pertinent."

Zach swore. "You're killing me."

"Hey, it's my day off. You're killing *me*. The only reason McCarthy called me is because he knows we're friends. You better know you'd have been arrested for disturbing the peace and interfering with an ongoing investigation if not for your connection to Laurel."

"I'm a Carson. Doesn't that mean your kind is always tossing mine in jail for no reason?"

"No real Carson was ever an FBI agent, that I can tell you." At Zach's scowl, Hart grinned. "Want to go play darts? Take your mind off it so you can work out the knots?"

Part of him did. It was something he and

Hart did often when Hart was stuck on a difficult case and needed something mindless to do. Maybe it was exactly what Zach needed. Maybe he could get somewhere on this whole mess if he just separated himself from it for an hour or so.

But Daisy was back there and something had to be done. She couldn't spend the night there. Even with these two guys locked up, more would be coming. More might be on their way, and while Zach could lock them up in that building pretty tightly—anything could happen.

Damn, but he needed some answers. "Can't. Got work."

Hart nodded. "I'll leave you to it. Just leave the deputies alone."

"You going to pass along whatever information you find out?"

"Night, Simmons," Hart said, opening his car door and sliding inside.

Zach sighed but he dug his keys out of his pocket and walked to his car. He *could* keep pounding at the deputies, but they wouldn't budge. And the more he did, the less chance he had of sneaking some information out of Hart later.

He didn't have time for either, though. Action was required. Cam wouldn't approve of the idea forming, which meant Zach would need to be especially sneaky.

He drove back to the house, watching for tails, taking the long, winding way and missing the turn off the highway twice and doubling back before he was satisfied no one had followed him.

He parked his car back in the hidden garage, though he wondered if it should be easier to access.

Well, not if he could get his plan wheels turning ASAP. He'd need to get rid of Cam and Hilly first.

He texted Cam that he was disengaging the security from the outside and coming in. Then set about to do just that. When he finally stepped into the common room, Daisy jumped to her feet from where she'd been seated at the table.

"Oh, my God. You're hurt."

It startled him, the gentleness mixed with horror in her tone. Like she cared. She even rushed over to him and touched the corner of his mouth, which was a little swollen from the elbow he'd gotten there.

"I'm all right," he managed, his voice rusty. "Just a tussle." He ste/pped away from her too soft and too comforting hand. "I need to get the security systems—"

"I'll get them running," Cam said, holding up Zach's phone. He went to work and Zach turned back to Daisy.

She looked pale. Exhausted.

"Thanks for your help, guys, but you should head home," he said to Cam and Hilly, keeping his voice neutral. "We'll all sleep and reassess in the morning."

Cam studied him, and Zach did his best to look blank. Cam couldn't know what he was planning. Not yet.

Cam handed the phone back and looked at Hilly. Something passed between them because Hilly nodded.

He'd never been able to communicate with anyone like that, and he wasn't sure if that was just the nature of never having been in a serious, committed relationship the way Cam and Hilly were, or some fundamental lack inside him.

Right now was certainly not the time to wonder about it.

"Show him the text message," Hilly said, laying a comforting arm on Daisy's shoulder before she passed by.

"What text message?" Zach demanded.

Daisy glared at Hilly, but Hilly and Cam slid out the door, clearly leaving Zach to handle it.

"Daisy. Show me the text message."

"It's nothing," she replied, but she picked up her phone, tapped a few things, then slid it his way. "Just Jordan being oh so very concerned."

Zach read the text message, scowled at the screen. "Where did he hear you're out of town?"

"Zach. I'm sure any number of people are saying that about me since I'm not home or touring or anything else."

But Zach didn't like it. For a wide variety of reasons he'd parse later, once he got his plan off the ground. "Does Jordan often contact you?" If this was out of the blue, it would give some credence to Jordan being involved.

"Not often. But a text message isn't out of the norm. Things like 'I'll be at x place on y date. I'd appreciate a lack of a scene.'"

Zach's mouth quirked, though he knew it shouldn't amuse him. "Let me guess. You caused three scenes."

She grinned at him, eyes sparkling. "How'd you know?" But she sighed. "I don't let anyone tell me what to do, most especially some *man* who thinks he has a right when he gave that up. And trust me, I want nothing more right now than to show up at his door drunk as a skunk. But I've learned not to give in to the impulse *every* time—because half the time it's a publicity stunt. He wants a scene from me so he can play the injured, horrified party."

A publicity stunt. "He wants to ruin you," Zach said flatly.

"He wants to make me look bad. I think there's a difference." She shrugged jerkily, pretending it didn't bother her. But he could see the bother written all over her tense posture and the way she gripped the phone. "The more I think about it, the more I can't pin him for this. He's too much of a narcissist. Nothing he does to me is trying to ruin me—he's just trying to help himself."

But a dead ex-wife could be helping himself, making him a sympathetic figure once again. And being a narcissist didn't make a person less likely to exact revenge if they felt they'd been wronged.

But he didn't need to argue with her or convince her of anything. Jordan was as high on his suspect list as her manager. He'd find out the truth and she'd deal with that one truth, instead of all the possible ones.

Weary, aching body, Zach lowered himself into one of the kitchen chairs. "Then your response should really stick it to him."

She looked at him sideways. "Go on."

"Verbal judo."

"What's verbal judo?"

"I won't give you the whole spiel, but basically it's a way of talking to people that neutralizes a confrontation."

"I don't want to neutralize it. I want to explode it."

"I know you do, sweetheart, but we're trying to give you a low profile."

"He expects me to explode. Shouldn't I give him what he expects? Just to keep him from looking too deeply into things? Or maybe even salvage some piece of my reputation."

Since Zach didn't believe Jordan was all that ignorant of what was going on, he merely shrugged. "You could, but he knows *something* is up. This is his version of fishing. So instead of giving him the reaction he wants, drive him crazy. Just say thank you for your concern. It gives away nothing. It harbors no ill will, and it admits no guilt. It'll probably eat him alive since he was clearly fishing for a reaction. It's *that* part I don't trust." Or the timing—reaching out just as two people trying to get to Daisy were taken into custody by police. Pretending he thought she was in rehab. Zach wasn't going to trust any coincidences.

Daisy stared at her phone, contemplating.

"You really think a response like that will eat him alive?"

"He knows you, right? Understands that you'll do the opposite of what he says, understands that any attempt at peace offerings will end with fiery explosions. So you don't give him what he wants."

"You make me sound like a shrew."

"No, I'm trying to make him sound like a jerk. Because he could just not. He doesn't need to reach out, doesn't need to poke at you. He could leave you be. But he's trying to piss you off, and so much worse than that, he's doing it under the guise of concern. Don't give him the satisfaction, because trust me, he's getting some satisfaction over that or he wouldn't be reaching out."

She contemplated her phone, then she picked it up and began to type.

Thanks for your concern!

She angled the screen toward him. "Is the exclamation point too much?"

"I think it works."

"Send," she said, tapping the screen with a flourish. Then she sighed and stared at him, her eyes lingering on the split lip and the bruising along his jaw. "I thought you were convinced Stacy was the culprit."

"I'm not convinced anyone is the culprit. We're looking into any possibility." And they needed to find them sooner or later.

He opened his mouth to tell her the rest of his plan, but she moved over to him and touched the part of his cheek that throbbed. Everything inside him tangled tight. She studied him, her fingers gently tracing over the line of his bruised jaw.

If he'd known what to expect, he might have been able to ward it off, but her gentleness undid him. Magnetized him. He couldn't remember anyone... His life was taking care of people, finding out the truth, saving people when he could.

No one ever asked if it was a burden. He'd never wanted or needed anyone to comfort that burden. It was his.

But Daisy's touching him was being given a gift so perfect, he wouldn't have ever thought to ask for it.

She slid into his lap. He held himself still, even if with all that stillness a desperate desire rioted inside him. It wasn't like the other night, her trying to prove something, defuse something, or just forget her circumstances.

There was a sweetness to this, even as close as their bodies were. Even though she made him want her in totally unsweet ways. She was gentle. She was...caring.

"Daisy." It was a croak, but he didn't have the wherewithal to feel self-conscious over it.

"Shh." She pressed her mouth to the side of his, just the gentlest, featherlight brush. "Someone's got to kiss the hurts."

A breath shuddered out of him, and even though it was the absolute last thing he should do, he closed his eyes as she gently kissed all along the bruised portion of his jaw. It was comfort and it was relief, and he had no business taking it from her when he was supposed to be keeping her safe.

*Safe.* Not hiding in abandoned buildings while someone prowled *this close* to being able to touch her.

No, today he'd failed. There could be no more failure. Only action.

"We don't have time for this." Which wasn't precisely true, but it was a hell of an excuse because his willpower was fading.

"I think we have all the time in the world," she replied, pressing her mouth to his neck.

His vision nearly grayed before he had a chance to slide her off his lap. Dear *Lord*, was that hard to do. Harder to let her go after he nudged her back a pace.

But he did it. "Pack your bags, Daisy. We're headed to Nashville."

## Chapter Ten

Daisy felt…strange leaving Zach's little ghost town. Like she'd miss it. Which was crazy since she'd been cooped up in that odd little house, not out enjoying the blue sky or mountains in the distance or in this very early morning's case, the stars out in their full and utter splendor.

Nothing had been good here, and yet she didn't want to leave. Didn't want to face Nashville or the people she knew, even with Zach at her side.

Because facing meant accepting that someone she loved and trusted might be behind this.

But she didn't argue. She'd packed her bags like Zach had said. She'd enjoyed maybe thirty seconds of looking up at the vast universe before Zach had whisked her into his car and started the drive.

He'd said nothing about the kisses, but for a few moments he'd relaxed under her.

She smiled a little to herself. Well, not *all* of him had relaxed.

She gave him a sideways glance. He was driving to some tiny independent airport in some other part of middle of nowhere Wyoming, where they'd fly in some tiny little plane to a few airports all the way to Nashville.

Nashville. It wasn't home, because she didn't particularly feel like she *had* a home. She'd been touring since she could remember, only ever staying with Mom and Vaughn for bits of time. As an adult she'd bought a house in Nashville, but she'd sold it when she'd married Jordan.

Then they'd sold the house they'd bought together. The house she'd thought she'd start a family in, have a life in.

"You know, I don't have a place in Nashville," she said after a while.

"I do."

"You have a place in Nashville?" she asked incredulously. She'd believed he knew enough people to take a small plane halfway across the country, but this seemed far-fetched. And yet, she trusted him implicitly, regardless of what seemed believable.

"I know people, Daisy. I found us a safe place to stay."

She kept staring at him, because something about the split lip and the bruising on his face—even with the dark five-o'clock shadow over it, made her feel safe even when she knew she wasn't.

But Zach would protect her, no matter the circumstances. Even though she knew Zach was human and that anyone could reach her if they wanted to badly enough, someone would fight to keep her safe.

Take blows. Give blows. For her.

He could push her away or insist they didn't have time for more than a kiss, but one thing Daisy knew was that Zach wasn't stoic or unaffected. He was worried about getting emotionally invested because he was already on his way to getting emotionally invested.

The thought cheered her enough that she dozed off, until Zack was waking her up with her real name again.

"Sleepy you doesn't seem to answer to the name Daisy," he offered, his voice rough with exhaustion and yet his lips curved.

"That's because Daisy Delaney doesn't sleep."

"All right, Lucy Cooper. You should really talk to that alter ego of yours, because you could both use some sleep." He gave her head a little pat and then slid out of the car.

She could only stare after him. There was something about the way he said her given name. It slithered through her, a not totally comfortable sensation—because it was too big for her skin. It made her heart swell and her eyes sting.

Jordan had never called her Lucy, even after she'd asked him to. Because she didn't want to be Daisy Delaney to her *family*. She'd wanted to separate it all out.

He hadn't understood.

Zach probably didn't, either, but he still used her name as though it didn't matter what he called her—she was the same. Not two identities fighting for space.

He opened the passenger door and looked at her expectantly. Right. She was supposed to get out of the car, not get teary over something so stupid.

"You haven't told me what the plan is," she said as she got out of the car. He grabbed their bags out of the trunk and headed for a squat little building.

The sun had risen, but it was still pearly morning light. And they had a long way to go to reach Nashville.

"Well, first we'll go see your manager."

"Together?"

He shrugged. "I don't see why not. You'll just tell people I'm your bodyguard." He walked to the building and knocked on the door, waiting for an answer.

When a scrawny young man answered he greeted Zach by name. They conversed for a while and then the young man led them through the office and out a back door.

Daisy felt like she was in a dream, complete with a tiny plane that made her breath catch in her lungs.

It didn't look safe, and if she'd been with anyone else she would have brought that up. But Zach would never take risks with her—that she knew. It had to be safe.

For a tin can hurtling through the air.

Zach helped her up the stairs and gave her hand a squeeze. "Afraid of flying?" he asked empathetically.

"I never have been before." She looked around the tiny cabin. "This plane changes things a bit."

"We'll be fine," Zach assured, and she was sure he thought so. She wasn't sure he was *right*, but she knew he believed he was. He gestured her into a seat and she took it.

"Why are we going to Nashville now?" Because if he talked maybe she wouldn't feel like running screaming in the opposite direction.

"Waiting isn't working. We're not getting closer—the trouble is only getting closer to you, and without warning. So we go straight to the potential leaks. We ferret them out. Besides, this way the rehab rumor can't really get anywhere."

He fastened her seat belt for her as she only stared, that same feeling from before—heart too big, skin too small.

She swallowed, trying to sound normal or just *feel* normal. "What does my reputation matter?"

"Jordan's taken enough from you, and whoever is behind this has taken even more. You don't need to give them pieces of yourself, too. We'll nip any rumors in the bud, and we'll find out the leak in one fell swoop."

No one had ever cared how many pieces she gave of herself as long as they got the pieces they wanted. Even Vaughn, for all his wonderful qualities, didn't understand her enough to do more than worry about her safety.

So she did the only thing she could think to do. She leaned over and pressed her mouth to his. She smiled against his mouth when he kissed her back for a brief second, then stiffened and eased her away.

Oh, he wanted her. She thought he might even *like* her.

"You have to stop doing that," he said sternly.

She did it again, a loud smack of a kiss, though this time he was tight-lipped and less than amused. Still, she flashed him a grin. "Stop kissing me back and maybe I will."

He didn't say anything to that, which made her settle back into her seat with a smile.

SHUTTLING ON AND off planes was exhausting. Add to that, Zach hadn't slept—not since the night before. But he drove the rental car through Nashville to the little farmhouse on the outskirts that one of his law-enforcement friends used as a safe house sometimes.

Daisy would like it. Somehow, he knew that. But he hadn't been prepared for the way her delight wound through him.

"Oh, my God! A chicken coop!" She jumped out of the car and practically ran over to it, leaning over the fence around the fancy little coop. He didn't see any chickens, but the gray, cloudy skies were spitting out a drizzle that probably kept the animals safe in shelter.

"My friend says there's a list of chores to do, if you're into that kind of thing."

She turned to look at him, eyes bright and

smile wide. "Are you kidding? Why didn't you bring me *here* in the first place?"

He didn't mention it had been because he didn't trust most of the people in Nashville who had any connection to her. Her brother had wanted to isolate her to keep her safe.

It had been a failure of a plan—Zach's own fault for not seeing the holes in it.

He shook that failure off—had to until the job was done—and focused on the new plan. "I do want you to give your manager a call and tell her you're planning to come into town tomorrow. Tell her you want a meeting, morning or afternoon doesn't matter, but I want her to believe you're leaving in the evening."

"And are we keeping this meeting?"

"Of course."

Some of her simple joy over the chicken coop had faded, but she didn't argue with him. Didn't try to tell him for the hundredth time she trusted her manager. "And…"

She trailed off, turning her gaze back to the chickens. He couldn't read her feelings from just looking at her back, but he thought the fact she was hiding her face told him enough to gather she wasn't happy.

"You'll be with me, right?"

"You aren't going any damn where without me, sweetheart."

She turned to face him again, lifting an eyebrow. "Oh, is that so?"

"You're not going to be contrary over that. Not right now. This isn't about telling you what to do. It's about keeping you safe. You and me are stuck like glue."

She smiled sweetly—which should have been his first clue something was off, but he was dead on his feet. She sauntered over to him, chickens forgotten. She reached out, and he stiffened against the touch.

Not that it didn't shudder through him as she playfully walked her fingers up his chest. He tried to ward it off, but then she looked up at him under her lashes.

"Like glue? What kind of sleeping arrangements were you planning?"

Lust jolted through him so painfully it was a wonder he didn't simply keel over. Or give up...and in to her.

But he wouldn't. He couldn't. "We'll figure it out inside."

"Don't tease, Zach." She sighed heavily, lifting her palm to his cheek.

It was becoming too common, too much of a want to have her hands on him. Still, he couldn't move away, could barely hold himself back from leaning in.

"You need to sleep."

"Safety first."

She looked around the picturesque yard. Even with the drizzle falling, it had a cheerful quality to it. Green grass and trees, red chicken coop and barn bright and clean in the rain. It was the complete opposite to the desolate, decaying place he'd originally taken her to.

It felt weirdly symbolic, only he was so exhausted he didn't know if it was good or bad. He ushered her inside with the security information his friend had given him. He dropped the bags and followed the email instructions on how to set all the security measures for the house.

"What's the best way for you to contact your manager?"

She eyed him and he had to stifle a yawn, had to work to keep his eyes open.

"In this case I think I need to call her. She'll have to rearrange her schedule to see me, I'm sure. She'll do it, she'll want to, but we'll have to work out the when and where."

"Okay. So, you'll call and set up a meeting." There'd be security to worry about— if the leak was through her manager's office someone would know she was there and accessible. "Make sure she doesn't think you're getting in until tomorrow, and thinks you're leaving in the evening."

"Okay. Can I make the call in private or do you need to listen in and make sure I'm a good girl who follows instructions?"

He wasn't sure what that edge in her tone meant, so he decided to ignore it. He made sure he held her gaze and didn't yawn, though one was threatening. "I trust you. There are three bedrooms. Take your pick. Just give me the time when you're done."

She stared back at him for a few humming seconds. He thought about the plane, when she'd kissed him and he'd been stupid enough to kiss her back.

Even though intellectually he knew it was a failure to get emotionally tangled with her, that it would put her in danger—put them both in danger. Though he never forgot how emotional entanglements had almost caused so much loss last year, he couldn't seem to help it. He was emotionally tangled.

There had to be a way to block it off. He knew better now. His brother was in a psych ward, and Cam had almost died. There were *costs* to an emotional connection—and if he couldn't control the connection, he had to find a way to keep it separate and make sure it didn't affect the case.

He knew better now, didn't he?

"You don't want a play-by-play of the phone conversation?" she asked after a while.

"The time will be enough." Because he had to focus on the facts of the case. The facts of what it would take to protect her. Enough with his precious patterns and trying to understand her and her life. He had to focus on the *facts*.

If he'd pulled her into more danger by bringing her closer to her stalker, he didn't have room for anything else.

Eventually, she nodded, picked her bag up off the floor and went in search of a room.

Zach picked up his own bag and pulled out his laptop. Before he could fall into blissful sleep, he had some work to do.

He'd been ignoring his phone for most of their travel, so he turned that on while he booted up his computer.

He winced a little at the ping of voice mails and text messages that sounded a few times. Yeah, a couple of people weren't too happy with him or his disappearing act.

He didn't bother to read all the text messages, and he deleted all the voice mails from Cam and Hilly without listening. But he did read the most recent text from Cam.

I hope you know what you're doing, because your client—you know, the guy paying us— isn't too thrilled.

So Zach would tell Daisy to contact her brother. Except, Texas Ranger or not, couldn't the leak just as easily be on his side?

Better to play this out as secretly as possible even if it meant everyone was angry with him. He'd suffer some ire to keep Daisy as safe as possible, and the best way to keep her safe was to test every possible leak in isolation.

So he didn't respond to Cam's text and went ahead and turned his phone back off. He needed to outline a plan for tomorrow.

He'd just close his eyes for a second, recalibrate the plan in his head, then formalize his hazy plan into something more specific. More...something.

The next thing he knew, someone was taking his hand. "Come on, sleeping beauty," an amused voice said.

He couldn't manage to open his eyes, but he was being pulled to his feet. Everything seemed kind of dim and ethereal. It was probably a dream.

Yes, he was dreaming Daisy was taking him somewhere, nudging him onto a bed, slipping the shoes off his feet.

He really was dreaming that after a while she curled up next to him, rested her hand on his heart and brushed a kiss across his cheek.

And since it was a dream, he let himself relax into it. Place his hand over hers, pull her curled-up body closer to his and settle into sleep.

# Chapter Eleven

Daisy wasn't sure what had compelled her to climb into bed next to Zach. He wouldn't appreciate it when he woke up. But she felt safer here, nuzzled against him, than anywhere else.

Talking to Stacy had been an exercise in torture. Daisy had wanted to tell her friend what was really going on, but all she'd been able to do was vaguely apologize for disappearing and ask for a private meeting, trying to evade Stacy's questions.

Daisy had read into every pause, every question. Was Stacy the one who wished her harm? Would this meeting end up being dangerous?

She swallowed against the lump in her throat and focused on Zach. The room was dark, but the glow from a bedside alarm clock was enough to illuminate his profile. His big hand over hers.

She felt safe with Zach. Not just the whole

"in danger with a security expert and former FBI watching out for her" thing, but she felt…emotionally safe with him. Which was weird. She didn't even feel that with Vaughn or Mom. She felt she had to be careful around them, because she'd followed Dad's footsteps and they hadn't approved—even if they loved her, they didn't *understand* her.

She wasn't certain Zach did, but so far it sure felt that way.

*And are you really stupid enough to think Zach is different than all the other men who've let you down?*

Except she'd watched Vaughn fall in love with Nat, the way it had changed him, opened him up. Because good men existed. She just hadn't known very many. Could she really trust her own judgment that Zach was one?

Except here she was, curled up next to him, with none of those doubts that had plagued her with Jordan. She didn't doubt Zach. He didn't make her doubt.

She let that thought lull her to sleep. She awoke to the jerk of his body, and male cursing. She smiled before she opened her eyes.

"I fell asleep?" Zach demanded, practically leaping out of bed. Outrage and sleep roughened his voice. She tried to press her lips together so she didn't smile, but she failed.

"Yeah, you were kind of dead on your feet, cowboy," she offered, stretching lazily out across the bed. "I tried to wake you up, but the best I could do was half drag you to bed. I didn't take advantage, though."

He gave her a sidelong look. Then he scrubbed his hands over his face and through his hair. Her fingers itched to do the same to him, but she knew Zach would want to right himself and get to work.

And quite frankly her heart felt a little soft, waking up next to him—even with the jolting wake-up. She wanted to wake up next to someone, which was not a new dream or fantasy, but it was certainly even more compelling with Zach as that someone.

"The meeting with Stacy is at eleven."

"Eleven?" He swore again. "That only gives us about two hours to plan."

"Why don't you take a shower, and I'll make coffee. Then we can plan." She didn't wait for him to agree before she slid out of bed and started heading for the door. She needed…coffee. A little coffee would steady the fluttering feeling in her chest.

But Zach stopped her on her way out of the room—a hand to her shoulder—and the flutters only intensified. He stared at her for the longest time, his big, warm hand resting on her shoulder.

"Whoever is behind this is to blame for all of this, no matter how much you trusted them. You can worry about a lot of things, but I don't want you worrying that you should have seen through someone."

Was that the fear inside her? Maybe. Whether it was Jordan or Stacy, part of her didn't want to know because then it would mean she was wrong.

At least she already knew she'd been wrong about Jordan. Maybe she'd root for him to be the person who wanted to hurt her. Except… She'd still feel stupid. Stupid and guilty that Tom's life was lost over something so…

Zach pushed a strand of hair behind her ear, sending a shiver of delight down her spine. Easing some of that band around her lungs. "We're going to figure this out, and then you're going to go back to your life. I promise you that." He smiled, a small smile meant to reassure. "And now that I've actually slept, no one's about to stop me. Trust that."

"I do," she whispered with far too much emotion. More than the situation warranted. But he made her feel all of these things she'd yearned to feel her whole life. Only music had ever soothed her this way. Only music had ever given her a sense she deserved anything good.

Here was Zach. Good, through and through, standing there close enough to lean in to. To kiss. To believe in.

She cleared her throat and took a step away. It was one thing to kiss him when she was trying to get under his skin, or forget about all the things wrong with her life right now. It was another thing to kiss him when she felt this...vulnerable.

She turned and walked carefully to the kitchen. She poked around until she found the coffee. It was percolating when Zach came out of the room they'd slept in, showered and dressed. He'd shaved, and the ends of his hair glistened.

It wasn't just lust that slammed through her. It was something so much bigger than that. Which kept her from acting on the lust.

She cleared her throat and placed a full mug on the table. "Here. I already put way too much sugar in it."

"Thanks." He placed his laptop on the table, slid into the seat, drank a careful sip. "Perfect."

And this was far, far too domestic for her poor heart right now. "So what's the plan?" she asked, sliding into her own chair. She was in danger. *That* was a far more important, and in weird, emotional ways, safer, topic.

"We'll go into the meeting together. You can introduce me as your bodyguard. No names, that way we don't have to remember a fake one. You'll say you're worried about your safety, but you really think your reputation needs a few shows to prove you're not in rehab."

"Like I said before, that'd go through my booking agent."

"Right. We'll stick with a version of the truth. You don't trust anyone else right now. You want to work everything out through her. Maybe it's not her normal job, but she could do it with extenuating circumstances."

"I guess so."

"As casually as you can, mention how you're heading home tonight."

"I don't have a home," she returned, too soft to make a joke out of it.

But Zach didn't even blink. "Who knows that?"

"What do you mean?" she asked, trying to drink enough coffee to chase away her dogged exhaustion.

"I mean, who of our suspects would say you don't have a home? Would Jordan?"

"He'd probably say Nashville. Home is where the career is, after all."

"And Stacy?"

"She'd probably say Texas, since my brother is there and she knows how much he and his family mean to me."

"Okay, there's a flight to Austin at ten. So you mention you're heading home tonight. If Stacy or someone on her staff heads to Texas, we know it's her. If Jordan starts poking around Nashville, we have reason to suspect him."

"How will you know all that stuff?"

Zach shrugged, tapping away at his computer. "It's not a perfect plan, but I've got eyes and I've got ears." He took another sip of his coffee then looked over the table at her. "All you have to do is talk to her like you normally would."

"But I don't feel normal. The phone was bad enough. In person?"

"In person, I'll be there. I can talk for you if need be. Just pretend to be overwrought."

"I'm never overwrought," she replied, but she kind of wished she could be. Wished she could hand it all over to Zach and let him take care of it. But no matter what he'd said about it not being her fault, this was her doing. Some choice in her life had made this happen.

She had to stand on her own two feet to fight it.

ZACH KNEW DAISY was nervous. It radiated off her as they slid out of the rental car, three blocks away from Stacy's office building.

Still, Daisy had that chin-in-the-air determination pushing her forward, and she didn't hesitate to walk with him. She didn't let those nerves overcome her.

Zach scanned the sidewalks, the buildings, the people who walked in front of them, as they zigzagged their way to the office building. He kept close to Daisy, hand always ready to grab his concealed weapon if need be.

But he didn't see or sense a tail. He'd expected to. It was a relief, though, and sadly not just for Daisy's safety. If he could scratch her manager off the suspect list he knew it would take a weight off her shoulders.

Zach opened the front door to the office building and gestured Daisy inside. For the remainder of the time he didn't walk by her side, but at her back, as most bodyguards would.

They rode the elevator in silence and walked down another hall without a word. Daisy's demeanor changed from vibrating nerves to cool determination, and that struck him as sadder somehow. How hard she was trying.

He noted every name on every door or sign, would write them all down after. Investigate any possible connections. Even though he shouldn't hope for any particular outcome because it would cloud his judgment, he hoped he could prove Stacy had nothing to do with anything.

As they entered the office labeled *Starshine Management*, a young woman behind a big desk immediately jumped to her feet with a bright smile. "Ms. Delaney! It's been so long."

"Hi, Cory. I've got a meeting with Stacy."

"Of course. Of course. Oh, my gosh, though, Ms. Delaney. I have to tell you, 'Put a Hex on My Ex' is getting me through a really tough breakup. I swear. I don't know what I'd do without your music."

Daisy smiled tightly. "You'd muscle through, but isn't it great we can have music to ease our hurts?"

"That's *exactly* right. I'll get Ms. Vine now." She grinned and bopped down the hallway before disappearing into an office with the blinds of the big glass front windows closed.

Daisy's expression melted into sadness. Worry.

"I'm not familiar with 'Put a Hex on My Ex.'"

Daisy's mouth quirked as he'd hoped it might. "Not many people are. It was on my first album after I stepped away from my dad's label and people didn't quite jump on the bandwagon right away. Not my most popular hour, though I love that song. Even more now."

He'd meant to change the subject, but it brought up an interesting point he'd overlooked. "Did you write your own music with your dad's record label?"

Daisy rubbed a hand to her temple and closed her eyes. "A few songs, I guess. Though I had cowriters with all of them, I think."

It was an angle he hadn't looked into enough—that someone who might want to hurt her might have a connection not just to her, but to her father. "Did Stacy have any connection to your dad's label?"

"Yes. She was an assistant. I convinced her to leave and take me on as her first client."

Could that be the connection? But he didn't have time to press her for more details because a woman who didn't appear much older than Daisy stepped out with the perky secretary.

"Daisy! *God.* I've been worried sick." She

engulfed Daisy in a hard hug before giving Zach a lifted eyebrow perusal.

"This is my bodyguard," Daisy said with a dismissive wave. "You know how my brother worries."

Stacy slipped her arm around Daisy's waist and started leading her down the hall. "Well, as he should. I'm so sorry this is happening to you, Daisy. What can I do?"

"I was hoping you'd ask that."

They were led back to Stacy's office, big and spacious, with a large window letting in a lot of light. Stacy didn't settle in behind the giant desk, instead taking an armchair that faced the one Daisy slid into.

They opened with small talk about mutual acquaintances, and Zach didn't notice anything odd about Stacy's demeanor. She acted like a friend, a concerned one, and a businesswoman invested in her client's career.

Daisy, to her credit, seemed perfectly relaxed, but there was just *something* about the way she held her purse in her lap that kept him from believing the act.

Daisy went through everything he'd tasked her with bringing up. The potential of a small, intimate concert with lots of security to promote her next single, the fact she was going to go home to relax for a few days. Asking Stacy to keep that last part secret.

"Daisy. Are you sure everything is okay? You don't seem like yourself."

"Would you seem like yourself if you'd found your bodyguard dead?"

Stacy winced. "I'm sorry. I'm just worried." Stacy gave Zach a cursory glance. "Not just for your safety, but for *you*. Are you sure you want to do any kind of performance with this going on? We can't exactly background check fans. I know you want to promote the album, but—"

"Wait. Why do you assume the person who killed Tom is a fan?" Daisy asked, and there was dismay clear as a bell in her voice.

Stacy blinked, all wide-eyed innocence Zach didn't know whether or not to believe. "Who else would it be?"

A loud siren interrupted the conversation, making all three of them jump at the jarring blast of sound.

Stacy frowned, glancing around the office. "What terrible timing for a fire drill," she called over the blaring noise.

Stacy looked uneasy, Daisy even more so. As for Zach himself, he didn't trust the timing at all.

"We should evacuate," he offered, holding

out his hand for Daisy to take. "What route would you normally take for a fire drill?"

Stacy shrugged helplessly, getting to her feet. "I... I don't remember. The stairs, obviously. Outside the doors. Then out the front? Or is it the back? Cory would know."

Zach nodded grimly, keeping his grasp on Daisy firm as he led her to the door.

Cory was standing in the middle of the office's waiting area, a bunch of things in her hands. She glanced back at them, worry and confusion replacing her previously cheerful expression. "I don't know what to grab and what to leave and—"

"I'm sure it's just a drill..." But Stacy's words trailed off as Cory pointed to the hallway outside the glass doors of the office. Smoke snaked across the floor.

"Come on," Zach ordered, pulling Daisy for the door. "Keep low. Evacuate the building in the most efficient way possible."

"Someone should call 911," Cory said, her voice trembling as Zach opened the door and pointed Stacy and Cory out, keeping Daisy next to him.

"We'll call when we're out. The most important thing is getting outside right now."

Stacy and Cory seemed totally helpless in

the hallway, staring at each other as smoke continued to snake around them.

"Follow us. Form a chain," Zach ordered, keeping Daisy's hand in his as he led them toward the staircase he remembered seeing.

The stairs were worse when it came to the smoke, but there was no heat—no flame that he could see. There weren't sprinklers going off, and Zach had a bad feeling it wasn't a fire so much as a distraction. Or a diversion.

Once they made it down the stairs, the lobby was filled with even more smoke, thick and acrid.

Daisy was tugging against his grip. He looked over his shoulder, but the smoke was thick enough he could only barely make her form out behind him. He didn't want to speak, trying to avoid inhaling as much as possible. But she kept pulling, harder and jerkier.

He nearly lost his grip on her, squeezing it tighter at the last moment and giving her a jerk toward him. "Stay with me," he ordered, and began pulling her through the smoke.

"Wait," she croaked.

But they were wading through smoke in a dangerous situation and he would most assuredly not wait.

He got them out of the building, milling crowds pushing at them the minute they stepped outside. Still, he kept pulling her, weaving through the crowd and away from the building.

"Zach! I lost my hold on Stacy. We have to go back," Daisy said desperately, her voice raspy from smoke.

Zach didn't stop moving or pulling her along. "They're fine. I don't think it's a fire. Now, what the hell was that stunt? Pulling on me that way? If I'd lost my grip on you—" He glanced back when she hacked out a cough.

Tears were streaming down her face, and his heart twisted painfully in his chest at her misery.

"It was Stacy," she offered weakly. "She kept grabbing and pulling at me in the opposite direction. I think she knew a better way out."

Zach nearly stopped cold, but the smoke and chaos reminded him to keep moving— with Daisy firmly in his grasp. "She did what now?" he demanded. It was easier to move faster out here where there was less of a crowd, so he hurried.

"I'm sure it was an accident. She was panicking and thought we needed to go in the other direction. But when you pulled on me, she lost her grip. She and Cory went out the back way, I think."

Zach shook his head, pulling her toward where they'd parked the car blocks away. He wanted to protect her from the truth, but he couldn't. It wasn't his job. "That doesn't look good for Stacy, Daisy. That wasn't a fire. It was smoke bombs, or something similar. Someone was trying to create a diversion. Someone knew you were coming and wanted to get to you, and it looks like Stacy was trying to help someone do just that."

# Chapter Twelve

Daisy didn't talk on the drive home. The pretty little farmhouse didn't cheer her up at all. She went straight to the bathroom and got into a steaming-hot shower and cried herself empty.

She'd trusted Stacy with her *life*. Everything Daisy had built for herself had been done with Stacy at her side.

She wanted to believe it was panic that had made Stacy try to pull her in the opposite direction of Zach. Maybe there was some explanation, but they hadn't stuck around to get it. Maybe she could still believe Stacy only *looked* guilty accidentally. Nothing was proven. Nothing was sure.

Except Zach, who was most definitely sure Stacy was involved.

Daisy half wished someone would just *do* something to her. At least it would be over then.

But that thought made her feel sick to her

stomach. She didn't want to be harmed or worse, even if it ended this waiting game. Upset and alive was better than at peace and dead.

She got dressed in comfortable pajamas even though it was only late afternoon. Part of her wanted to sleep until this whole thing was over. It wasn't possible, but maybe for tonight while she came to grips with how bad this looked for Stacy's connection to everything.

She stepped out of the bathroom, tempted to head into the room she'd put her stuff in yesterday. Which was not the room she'd spent the night in with Zach.

Zach. She couldn't shut him out even though she wanted to. He was trying to keep her safe, determined to. It wasn't his fault she apparently had terrible judgment when it came to people. It wasn't his fault the people she thought were trustworthy and honest were potentially wishing her harm.

So she forced herself to walk back out to the pretty little living room. It reminded her of something out of *Little House on the Prairie*, but there was a sheen of cleanliness and chicness to it. It was its own little fantasy world, and boy, could she use a fantasy world.

Complete with hot protector guy standing

in the kitchen cooking. No doubt making her dinner. No doubt he'd watch like a hawk to make sure she ate.

When he turned to glance at her, there was sympathy there. It made her throat close up all over again. She didn't want to cry in front of him, though, much as she knew he'd comfort her and be perfectly sweet about it.

She wanted to be strong, not to prove something to him, but to herself. That a fleeting thought about wishing someone would just end things didn't mean she particularly wanted to be ended.

"So that was more eventful than I thought it would be." She settled herself onto a stool at the counter that separated the kitchen from the dining area.

"That it was. I know it's hard for you to think Stacy could be a part of this, but we have to accept that possibility."

Daisy nodded, spinning her phone in a little circle on the counter. "Yeah. I get that."

"If it helps, I don't think she's acting alone. The hired muscle back in Wyoming, smoke bombs. She doesn't strike me as someone who could run a demanding business and plan all this. I think she might be a pawn."

"Oh, gee, more people out to get me."

"She might be an unwitting one."

"Whatever she is, she's connected." Even saying the words made Daisy's stomach twist. She kept thinking she'd accepted it, and if she accepted it she could move forward.

Except she couldn't accept it. Even when Zach was calm and reasonable.

"All evidence points to yes." Zach drained pasta in the sink with a deft hand.

"Where'd you learn to cook?" she asked, wanting to talk about anything other than Stacy.

"My mother. She believed in raising boys who could take care of themselves." Something on his face changed.

"Boys. You have brothers?"

"A brother."

"You've only mentioned Hilly and your murdered father. I didn't know there was a brother."

He shrugged. "Did you want my life history?"

Because the honest question hurt her more than it should, she smiled sharply at him. "Well, we did sleep together, sugar."

His mouth quirked as if he almost found her funny. "Uh-huh. Well, I have a brother."

"Is he Mr. Protector guy, too? Or are you more like me and my brother?"

"What's you and your brother?"

"Opposites, through and through."

"But you love him."

"Of course I do. Vaughn was one of the very few uncomplicated relationships in my life. Well, mostly uncomplicated. I always knew he didn't really approve of me, but he supported me anyway." She hadn't always appreciated that support the way she should have, and she'd never thanked him for it.

Although he'd be horrified by a display of emotion, even if it was gratitude. The thought made her smile a little bit. But she realized, as Zach placed a bowl full of spaghetti in front of her, he'd very efficiently avoided the question.

"So what does your brother do?"

"He's done a lot of things."

She raised an eyebrow. "You know, when someone touches a sore subject with me I tell them to jump off a cliff."

"And I doubt it dims their curiosity regarding the sore subject," Zach replied.

"Avoiding the question doesn't dim my curiosity."

"Ethan's in a psych ward. He, in fact, nearly murdered Cam."

"Cam, your business partner, Cam? The man marrying your sister?"

"The very same."

He really, *really* never failed to surprise her.

She might have thought him cold at the way he delivered that so emotionlessly, but his eyes didn't lie as well as the rest of him. The less sympathy she offered, though, the more he seemed to reveal to her. "Well. I can see why it's a sore subject."

"Dad's murder hit him particularly hard. He tried his hand at a lot of things, but the unsolved case was an obsession, one that became unhealthy and dangerous. I love my brother, even knowing his... I hesitate to call them faults. He's mentally ill. He's... Well, my attempts to protect him, to care for him, not only put the entire undercover FBI investigation I was a part of in jeopardy, but nearly got Cam killed, too. You learn from experiences like that. And, in my case, you get kicked out of the FBI."

"Which is why you shouldn't get emotionally involved," she said, remembering how seriously he'd asked her if she wanted to die after she'd kissed him that first time.

He tapped his nose, then focused on eating.

"It isn't the same," she said softly.

He raised an eyebrow, and somehow she'd known he'd give her that condescending look he thought hid all the turmoil inside him. Maybe he managed to hide it from other people, but not from her.

"You knew your brother had issues, and you kept protecting him until you didn't have a choice. That isn't the same as feeling something for me. Emotion didn't cause those mistakes. Underestimating your brother's illness and your power over it would have been the issue. It doesn't mean you'll make the same mistakes with me."

"Who says I won't?"

She blinked at that, more than a little irritated when her phone trilled. Downright furious when it was Jordan's number calling her.

"Why can't that bastard leave well enough alone?" she grumbled, reaching for the phone to hit Ignore.

"Take it," Zach said in that leader-ordering-a-subordinate tone that would have angered her more if she wasn't so confused.

"Huh?"

"Take it. See what he wants. On speaker."

She didn't want to talk to Jordan, not when she was getting somewhere with Zach. Not when today was already in the toilet. But she did as Zach ordered her to do because she didn't know what else to do in the moment besides stomp her feet and throw a tantrum like a child.

"Jordan," she greeted as coolly as she could muster.

"Daisy. Thank God you're all right."

Fear snaked through her. While Zach had told her the smoke bombs at Stacy's office had made the news, people had been distracted enough not to notice she'd been in the building. So far. "Why wouldn't I be all right?" she asked, trying to keep her voice devoid of emotion.

"The attack on Stacy's office! They're claiming it was an innocent prank, but this is all too close for comfort. I'm worried about you, Daisy. What kind of trouble have you been getting yourself into?"

She glanced up at Zach, who had that icy law-enforcement scowl on his face. But again, in his eyes she could see the truth. Heat and fury.

"You know I'm in town?" she asked carefully.

"I keep tabs, Daisy. I've told you that before." He sounded so disdainful she wanted to punch him. "I have to know if you're going to show up and make one of your scenes."

"But you said you thought I was in rehab."

"No, I said that's what people were saying, and that I hoped you were getting help. You need help."

*And you need a knee to the balls.*

"We need to talk, Daisy. In private. No staff. No bodyguards. I have some important news for you and I need to make sure you're going to handle it the correct way."

She opened her mouth to say she'd show him the correct way to handle something, but Zach reached across the counter and tapped her hand. He scribbled something onto a piece of paper then angled it toward her.

*Take the meeting.*

She jerked the pen from his hand and wrote her own note back.

*Without you?*

"Daisy? Listen. Meet me at our old lunch place. What do you say, eight o'clock before your flight?"

Daisy stared at Zach, who nodded emphatically. She let out a sigh. "Fine, Jordan. I'll be there at eight. Goodbye." She hit End on the call before he could say any more.

"Stacy had to have told him you were here. She's the only one who knew about that flight," Zach said, scribbling more things onto a new piece of paper. "There has to be a connection there."

"Between Stacy and Jordan? They didn't like each other. Trust me. Cory could have told him, too."

"Cory didn't know about your flight unless she was eavesdropping. Besides, Jordan and Stacy disliking each other isn't valid enough to disregard the potential connection. Because it doesn't have to be a connection of friendship, does it? The enemy of my enemy is my friend and all that—and before you say anything, I know Stacy isn't your enemy, but sometimes people harbor resentments we don't know about. You said she was at your father's label with you."

"No, she was my father's manager's assistant. We used to sit around and complain about what a smarmy old codger he was, so when I finally got the guts to go out on my own, I asked if she wanted to come with. We'd been friends, dreaming about futures where we didn't have to answer to anyone. Might have been tough work those first few years, but I'm pretty sure Stacy has been amply rewarded."

Zach paced. "None of this adds up," he muttered. "We're missing something." He tilted his head, clearly working something out in that overactive brain of his. "Or someone. What about someone who would know both Jordan and Stacy separately. Someone who who knows you well enough to use them both against you? Who in your life would know both Jordan and Stacy enough to understand their relationship to you?"

"My agent. Jordan's staff—his manager,

his assistant—basically anyone on his payroll who would have worked with Stacy during one of our joint ventures before the divorce."

"I looked into Jordan's staff before, but we'll go through them again. See if we can find a specific connection to Stacy. And then triangulate it to your father."

"And while you're doing all that?"

"You better get ready. Because you're going to have to hide some of your fury toward Jordan. Just long enough to get us through this meeting and get what we want out of it."

THE PATTERNS DIDN'T add up, but Zach was beginning to think he'd been looking at them all wrong. There were a lot of players, but no clear leader. No clear link.

If he could find the link, the pattern would fall into place.

Daisy didn't think anyone would have something against her writing her own songs, but Zach had to believe it was industry related. Jordan, the rising star. Stacy, the star's manager—who came from her father's record label.

"What about this manager? The one Stacy worked for."

"What about him?" Daisy asked, staring out the window as Zach drove through drizzly downtown traffic to the restaurant Jordan had picked out.

"Could he have been angry at you for stealing Stacy away?"

Daisy snorted. "He didn't care about Stacy. He cared about power."

"What does that mean?"

"Look, he'd be like…eighty now. I doubt he overpowered Tom and killed him. I doubt he'd have the wherewithal to follow me around the country."

"*He* isn't. Whoever is behind this is sending people, Daisy. What would this guy be angry about?" He didn't add *and why the hell didn't you tell me*, which he considered a great feat of control.

Daisy shifted in her seat. "Nothing. He got away with it all. There'd be nothing to be angry about."

"Got away with what exactly?"

She sighed heavily. "He just said some kind of inappropriate things and I told my dad about it. But it's not like… There was nothing to be angry about. Nothing happened to him."

Zach parked in the lot in front of the restaurant, then looked over at her. "*Said* some inappropriate things, or *did* some inappropriate things?"

She waved a hand and pushed the passenger door open. "Doesn't matter."

"It *does* matter," he insisted, but she got out of the car and started walking toward the door—which was not the plan they'd agreed on. He hopped out of the car, stopping her forward progress. "Follow the plan, Daisy. And tell me about it."

"It doesn't *matter*. Trust me. Nothing bad ever happened to him. If he's angry with me, it's not enough to want me hurt. Why would he be angry? He's old and rich and retired, I believe. Hell, he might even be dead. Whatever he is—he's fine, and not out to get me."

"Name."

"Oh, for God's sake, Zach. Can't you trust me?"

"I trust you implicitly. I don't trust anyone who would say or *do* inappropriate things to you when you were a teenager."

They couldn't keep having this conversation in public, even with her big sunglasses and baggy clothes.

"He grabbed me. I told him no. He grabbed me again. I said I was going to go tell my dad. He laughed and said Dad wouldn't do anything. And guess what? He was right. *Oh, Don's just old guard, Daisy girl. Don't be alone with him.* Problem solved, right?"

"The hell it is."

She shook her head, wrapping her arms around herself. "It was forever ago. It's ancient history."

It wasn't. He could tell it wasn't, but she didn't want to discuss it and here wasn't the place. "What about Stacy?"

"What *about* Stacy?"

"Did he assault Stacy, too?"

"He didn't *assault* me, Zach."

"Grabbing is assault, Daisy," he returned forcefully. But he softened because even for all the difficult situations he'd been in, he'd never had to mine through his past. Never had to wonder who was against him. He placed his hands on her shoulders. "I know it hurts. I can't imagine how much it hurts to wonder about everyone you trust, or everyone you don't want to have to think about. I wish there was some other way, but we're missing a link and the sooner I can find it, the sooner whoever is torturing you can be brought to justice."

"I just want this to be over. I'm not even sure I care about justice," she said, looking teary.

He let her lean into him. Rubbed his hand up and down her back. "I know. I know. One link. I just need one link and then I can connect it all. I can make it over for you. Let me follow this lead. A name, and all you have to do is—"

She lifted her head off his shoulder, and nodded behind him. "Have dinner with my ex-husband?"

Zach didn't turn. Instead, he kept his arm around Daisy, kept looking down at her. "We're going to play this a little differently than we planned."

"Oh, really?"

He dropped his head and brushed his mouth against hers, inappropriately enjoying that for once he'd been the one to surprise her with a kiss. "Not your bodyguard this time."

Her mouth quirked up. "Well, this should be interesting."

He slid his arm around her waist and turned to face Jordan Jones, who did *not* look happy to see them.

Zach grinned. "Indeed it will."

## Chapter Thirteen

Daisy's whole life, she'd prided herself on standing on her own two feet. Even when her father had been taking her from show to show as a little girl, she'd understood that it was necessary to prove a certain amount of independence so she didn't turn into her father's toy or trophy. If she hadn't inherently understood that, her mother had made sure to remind her.

Daisy had wanted to be a singer, and she'd become one. On her own terms. But there had been things that had undermined that independence, that certainty. Her father ignoring the fact his manager had—as much as she hated it, she'd use Zach's word—*assaulted* her. Jordan being...well, self-serving, she supposed.

Could she hate him for that?

"I thought we were going to have dinner, Daisy. I don't appreciate—" he trailed off, looking Zach up and down "—whatever stunt this is."

Turned out, she could hate Jordan for a lot of things. "No stunt. My boyfriend refused to let me out of his sight with everything going on." She patted Zach's chest. "He's very concerned about my well-being."

Jordan sighed, all long-suffering martyrdom. "If that's supposed to be a dig against me, perhaps I should apologize for treating you like an independent woman?"

*Perhaps you should apologize for being an emotionally abusive jerk wad.* But she smiled sweetly. "Jordan Jones, this is my boyfriend…" She tried to come up with a fake name, but Zach intervened.

"Zach Simmons," he offered, holding out a hand for Jordan to shake. "I'm in law enforcement, so I understand just how dangerous this threat against Lucy is. Her going anywhere alone wasn't a great idea. I'm sure you understand her safety is paramount."

It…warmed her somehow that he was using her real name, and his. Jordan probably wouldn't notice or care, but it was…a gesture.

"Well." Jordan straightened his shoulders. "Of course. That's what I wanted to talk to Daisy about. Her safety."

"Great!" Zach said so genially Daisy wanted

to laugh. "Let's head in." Zach kept his arm around her waist as he led them inside and told the hostess they had three in their party.

It was something to watch, how easily he could switch into someone else. A role. She understood that a little. After all, there was a certain amount of *role* she stepped into when she got on stage. Daisy Delaney was parts of Lucy Cooper carefully arranged into a different package.

But she'd really never expected too many other people to understand that. It had been part of the attraction of Jordan—that he understood the complications of being someone else at the same time you were yourself.

But she supposed there were all kinds of ways people put on masks every day, not just to go on stage.

The hostess led them to a dimly lit booth and Daisy had to fight the need to laugh hysterically. She was sitting in a restaurant with her ex-husband and her security expert slash fake boyfriend slash man she really wouldn't mind seeing naked.

While apparently, said man suspected both her manager and her ex-husband of stalking and murder.

Zach draped his arm over her shoulders easily, chatted with Jordan about the music industry. Daisy could hardly pay attention to Jordan's pretentious rambling about his career. Had she really been this *fooled*?

But she had been. Fooled or desperate or something. It made her feel sick and ashamed she hadn't seen through him—but he hadn't talked about himself back then. He'd talked about her. Flattered her—in just the ways she'd been desperate to be flattered.

A strange thought hit her sideways as Jordan nattered on. Could he have been coached? Told what would hit all her vulnerabilities, and then used them against her?

Oh, that was insane. Whatever was happening to her hadn't been going on for *years*. Her failed marriage was hardly some kind of convoluted plot to…hurt her or whatever. She was getting paranoid. Insane maybe.

"Which brings me to why I called," Jordan was saying, his gaze moving from Zach to Daisy. Pretty blue eyes the color of summer skies. She'd thought she'd seen love in them once, and she didn't know if she was just that delusional or if he had actually felt something for her and it had disappeared.

It made her unbearably sad. And then Jordan continued.

"The rumor *was* you'd disappeared to go

into rehab, and it got me thinking how great it would be if you just did that."

"What?" she replied, because surely he didn't mean what she *thought* he meant.

"You might want to work on your comedy, buddy. Because that isn't funny," Zach said, steel laced through his fake genial tone.

"Can I get y'all something to drink?" a perky waitress asked, clearly not reading the mood of the table.

They all ordered robotically, except Jordan, who smiled and flirted when the waitress recognized him and expressed her undying love for his music.

If she recognized Daisy, she didn't mention it.

When she disappeared to get the drinks, Jordan looked at them both with that patented *Jordan Jones* smile. It was charming, and he was handsome. She wanted to punch him in the nose, but Zach's arm around her shoulders had tightened as if keeping her seated.

"It seems to me a rehab facility would be safer than going around disappearing with—" he looked at Zach "—boyfriends. Especially the way your last one ended up."

"Tom was my bodyguard and he died trying to protect me, you inconsiderate—"

Jordan held up his hands, looking at Zach

with a sigh as if to say, *What do you do with a problem like Daisy?* "I'm only suggesting a safe place for you, Daisy."

"You want me to fake going into rehab so I can be *safe*?"

The waitress put glasses in front of them, and this time she gave Daisy a much longer look. Though she was smart enough not to say anything.

Jordan sipped from his glass. "I mean, you could actually go."

"I'm not an alcoholic, Jordan. Contrary to your staff's attempts to make me out to be."

"Of course. Of course." He opened his mouth to speak, but the phone he held in his hand trilled. He glanced at the screen, a slight frown pulling at the corner of his lips. "I have to take this," he said, sliding out of the booth. "If you'll excuse me." He moved away from the table and Daisy couldn't hear what he was saying.

"I can't believe you married this joker," Zach muttered when Jordan was out of earshot.

"*That* is not the joker I married." No, Jordan knew how to slip into a role, too. Was she forever falling for men who acted one way, then turned out to be another? "You know a little bit about pretending to be someone else to get what you want, don't you?"

He looked at her, something like sympathy in his gaze that made her want to punch him, too. Or lean into his chest. She really wasn't sure.

He reached out and pushed a stray strand of hair behind her ear. "All I want right now is to keep you safe."

Which softened her up considerably.

"Which means I'm going to get my hands on his phone."

"Huh?"

"I don't trust this rehab thing."

"He's just trying to make me look bad, Zach. Ever since I asked for a divorce, that's his number one goal. Because if he can make *me* look bad, he can make himself look better."

"Maybe. Maybe that's all it is, but he doesn't strike me as particularly smart. Manipulative, yes. A good actor? Sure. But someone is pulling his strings, Daisy. I'm going to find out who."

"It's got to be someone on his staff."

"I agree. His manager, maybe? Was there anyone he was particularly…deferential to?"

Daisy tried to think back over her time with Jordan. "I think he's been through something like three managers. He used to talk about some uncle who was in the industry, but I never met him. If he mentioned him by name, I don't remember him."

"I need his phone. So when I give you the signal, you're going to spill your drink on him. I'm going to palm his phone and head off to the bathroom to wash up."

"You're going to palm his phone? How?"

"Trust me." He smiled, tapping her nose. "If you do, maybe I'll teach you a few things about going undercover."

It amused her, even though all she really wanted was to have her life back. "You better be quick, though. His phone is like an arm. He'll notice it's missing."

"You just spill his drink. I'll handle the rest."

She did so, and beautifully. Perhaps with a little too much enjoyment as the dark soda splashed across Jordan's white shirt, but hell, Zach enjoyed Jordan's outrage a little too much himself.

Zach immediately jumped to his feet, calling for the waitress and shoving napkins at Jordan. It gave him ample time to slip the phone out of the sticky soda and pretend like he was going to run to the bathroom for more paper towels even though the waitress was hurrying over with a rag.

Zach moved quickly to the bathroom, locked himself into a stall and went to work on Jordan's phone.

Zach didn't have time to try and figure out Jordan's passcode, so he used a quick hack to bypass the code and get into Jordan's home screen.

He pulled up the contacts list. The first fishy thing was the lack of names. Everyone was labeled with letters and numbers rather than anything that helped Zach identify who they were. Pretty confusing for a guy who had tons of contacts in his phone.

And pretty damn suspicious. Zach pulled up the recent calls. With his own phone, Zach took a picture of the screen. Of the eight calls on top, two were repeated three times each. It might be nothing. It might mean everything. Now that he had the numbers, he'd go from there.

Text messages didn't reveal anything of importance, and his apps were as run of the mill as any. Zach didn't have time to dig further. Hopefully, the phone numbers would be something to go on.

He stepped out of the stall, wiped off the

phone with a paper towel and turned it off, ready to head back to the table. If Jordan had noticed his phone missing, Zach would just explain he'd gone to wipe it down and Jordan would be none the wiser.

But when he stepped back into the restaurant, the few patrons had their noses and phones pressed to every available window, and Daisy stood next to an empty table, hand to her mouth.

"What's going on?"

She gestured faintly at the window, but there were so many people crowded around it he couldn't see anything.

"The cops came and arrested him." Daisy looked up at him, searching for some kind of answer, but he was as confused as she was.

"The cops came in and arrested Jordan?"

She nodded. "A-at first it was just… They asked if they could speak with him outside. He looked so confused, but wholly unconcerned. I think he even thought maybe they were going to ask for his autograph or something, but instead… I looked out the window and he was being handcuffed. *Handcuffed.* Zach, it doesn't make any sense, and it's already being uploaded onto the internet in three million ways."

Zach looked down at the phone in his hand. "I guess I should give the cops his phone."

"Did you find anything?"

"I took some pictures of his recent call numbers, but if he's being arrested for something, the police should have it." He led Daisy outside through the small crowds of people, pushing his way through to the female cop holding the curious onlookers as far back as she could.

"Excuse me, Officer? I have Jordan Jones's phone right here."

The officer looked at him with a raised eyebrow as he held out the phone, but she didn't say anything.

"We had a little drink spill," Zach explained. "I cleaned off his phone for him. But figured you might want it."

"And you are?" the cop asked with no small amount of distrust.

Zach explained who he was, and the cop managed to escort him and Daisy to a slightly private corner. Zach showed the police officer all his identification and permits to prove he was Daisy's security, and gave an account of the drink spill.

The cop took and bagged the phone. "I

imagine our detectives will be in contact with you, Ms. Delaney."

"Can you tell me what he's being arrested for?"

The cop looked at Daisy, then him. "The murder of Tom Perelli."

Daisy audibly gasped, and Zach might have, too. *Jordan* as murderer? Even though he'd suspected Jordan was involved, it was hard to believe the man he'd just had dinner with was capable of murder.

But he didn't have time to dwell on that. Some people were beginning to look at Daisy and murmur among themselves. Phones began to move from the cop car where Jordan was now loaded up, to the dim corner where he and Daisy stood.

He moved his body to shield her from the prying eyes and phones, then discussed the best way to get out of the parking lot undetected. As the cop began to instruct the crowd to leave so she could back up the patrol car, Daisy and Zach slipped around the crowd and into Zach's car.

Daisy didn't say anything as they drove back. Zach couldn't read her mood, but he couldn't concentrate on it, either. He paid attention to every car on the road with them.

Quite frankly, he expected to be followed. He expected…something. Surely, this wasn't *it*. It was too easy, too neat. Something else had to be at work here.

But in the end they made it back to the farmhouse without any tail Zach could see. Once inside, he made as many calls as he could to weasel some information out of a few overly talkative individuals.

Daisy sat on the couch, staring at nothing. During one of his calls he'd fixed her some tea. She hadn't touched it.

After he'd gotten the answers he'd wanted, or at least *some* of the answers, he sat down next to Daisy. She didn't move. Didn't say anything. He supposed she was in shock.

"The police received an anonymous tip, which allowed them to obtain a search warrant for Jordan's place. They found the gun used to kill Tom in a hidden safe in his bedroom closet."

"Anonymous tip," Daisy echoed. "Someone else knew he… He couldn't have…" She swallowed. "Zach, I don't understand. I really don't. Maybe I could believe he stalked me, or even threatened me all those months, but to kill Tom? I can't…" She shook her head. "But it's over, isn't it? If Jordan is the murderer, and he's in jail, this is over."

Zach didn't know how to tell her he didn't

think it was over, that this was all too easy. And maybe it *was* over. Maybe it wasn't his gut telling him things were too neat. Maybe it was his desperate desire to be with her.

"Zach?"

She looked up at him, and in all that confusion and despair there was hope. Hope that this meant she got to go back to her real life and feel safe again. Hope that this could all be put away as some ugly part of her past.

For her, he wished he could believe it. Even if it meant their time together was up. She deserved to go back to normal, instead of living in fear.

"It's possible it's over," he said carefully, not wanting to burden her with his doubts. "Obviously, we'll want to see if they give him a bond. I'd hope not, but we want to make sure he's going to stay in jail before it's…fully over."

Daisy nodded, wringing her hands together. "I can't… I didn't know him. I thought I did. I loved the version of himself he showed me, but it wasn't him. I can't imagine him *killing* someone, but I certainly can imagine him wanting to hurt me."

She popped to her feet, began to pace. "He wanted me to go to rehab. He wanted me swept away so I wouldn't be credible. That's why he wanted to meet."

It was possible, Zach supposed. But the timing struck him as odd, even more so with the arrest in front of Daisy. Zach had some research to do on those numbers from Jordan's phone before he fully accepted this version of events. And he'd want to read the police report and—

"What about you?"

He looked up at Daisy, his mind going over all the things he still needed to do to be *sure*. "What about me?"

"You'll have to go home, then, won't you?"

It felt like a slap, even as she watched him with wide, sad eyes. He cleared his throat. She might have kissed him a few times, he might have grown to like her quite a bit, but their odd relationship was a temporary one.

He pushed away all those conflicting emotions that were no doubt clouding his judgment about Jordan's guilt. "My job is to keep you safe. Until we're assured Jordan stays in jail, that means I'm still here."

She nodded, gave him a tremulous smile that just about cracked his heart in two. "Good." When she sat, she didn't sit next to him. Instead, she slid onto his lap, much like she had way back in Wyoming.

She cupped his face with her hands, looked right at him. "Then be with me. Really."

# Chapter Fourteen

Daisy poured everything inside her into the kiss. The pain, the uncertainty, the horrible sadness that swept through her at the idea Zach wouldn't be in her life anymore.

She wasn't sure if it was the kiss that finally broke through Zach's whole "emotions are distractions" thing—because it was one hell of a soul-searing kiss—or if it was as simple as he believed this was over.

She wished she could, but everything felt wrong and off. Maybe she couldn't believe Jordan was a murderer because it made her look like a fool, but there were all these wiggles of uncertainty inside her she couldn't quash—even with Jordan in jail.

Zach's kiss could eradicate it, and all the other painful things inside her. She could focus on pleasure and the absolute safety she found in him and leave everything else behind, even if only for a little bit.

She thought she'd have to convince him, but his arms banded around her and his mouth devoured hers as if he hadn't rejected her attempts at this *routinely*.

He maneuvered her onto her back on the couch, sprawling himself over her so that she sank into the cushions. She reveled in that feeling of being covered completely, safe and complete somehow—like being in Zach Simmons's arms was exactly where she needed to be.

He kissed her like she was the same to him—the place *he* needed to be.

There were so many ways she'd been made to feel small and insignificant in her life by the men who were supposed to love her. Zach had never mentioned love, but he made her feel cherished and important more so than anyone else. He believed her, he trusted her, and time and time again he'd put her above his own interests.

She pulled his shirt off quickly and efficiently. She sighed reverently, tracing her fingers down his abdomen. "I've been waiting for this since I saw you shirtless that first night."

He muttered a curse and then kissed her again, a fervency and an urgency she appreciated because it seared away everything else—

all those awful things in the real world out there. It was only him and her, perfectly safe.

His hands streaked under her shirt and then pulled her up into a sitting position, his body straddling hers.

"If this is a curse, I'll damn well take it," he said, his eyes bright and lethal.

"Curse?"

"Carsons, Delaneys, long story." He closed his eyes and shook his head as if he couldn't believe he'd brought it up. "I'll tell you later." Then he lifted her shirt over her head and let it fall to the ground. His mouth streaked down her neck as his hands made quick work of her bra and she forgot her questions as he kissed her everywhere.

His groan of appreciation as he tugged the button and zipper of her jeans made her feel like a goddess. "One favor. Don't call me Daisy."

He paused briefly, then met her gaze as he pulled her pants down her legs. "All right, Lucy."

It squirmed through her—somehow beautiful and uncomfortable at the same time. But she didn't want to be Daisy to him, not because she was ashamed of that part of her, but because Daisy had to keep people at arm's length from all the demands inside her—from her music, from her drive to succeed, from the chaos that sometimes existed in her head.

But if she was Lucy, just herself without the mantle of fame or curse of being a storyteller, then she could feel like she really belonged to *him*. Not something bigger than them. Just them.

Zach stopped suddenly, keeping his body ridiculously tense. "Wait. Condoms. We don't—"

She patted his cheek. "Never fear, sweetheart, condoms and booze are two things I never leave home without."

"Do I even want to know why?"

"Sometimes a girl has a rep to protect. Or destroy, as the case may be. I like to be prepared."

"Well, I won't look a gift bad girl in the mouth. Wow, that sounds wrong."

She laughed, and was surprised to find it made the moment that much more special. That she could want him and laugh with him and feel safe with him. She brushed her mouth against his as she slid off the couch. "Come to bed, Zach."

He followed her and she rummaged through her bag, in only her underwear and socks. She might have felt a little silly if Zach wasn't watching her as though he'd like to devour her from top to bottom, then bottom to top.

That made her feel powerful no matter what she had on. She found the old crumpled box of condoms, discreetly checked the expiration date and then pulled one out, holding it between her fingers. "Aren't you lucky?"

"Yes," he said reverently, so reverently her eyes actually stung. She tried to saunter over to him, keep it light—focused on the attraction and the laughter, not...not the way her heart felt squeezed so hard she could barely catch a breath.

But when she reached him, she didn't know how to keep it all together. All she could do was lean against the warmth of his chest. Try to find some strength of spirit against that strong, dependable frame.

"I don't want this part to be over. The us part," she whispered, listening to the steady beating of his heart. She'd never, ever revealed herself like that before, laid her emotions that bare.

But she'd never let herself be Lucy with anyone outside her brother and her mother, and even they still saw her as part Daisy. Why she thought Zach understood the dichotomy inside her, she wasn't sure. Maybe she was stupid—the kind of stupid who married a murderer and—

He swallowed and ran a hand over her hair. Sweet and full of care. "Lucy," he said raggedly.

She shook her head against that despair in his voice. "I know. It's impossible. And God knows I shouldn't trust my own instincts when it comes to men. Maybe you're a secret murderer, too. How would I know?"

She wanted to run away, but Zach pulled her back and took her face in his hands.

"Lucy," he repeated, quieting her. She still felt wound up and stupid, but his hands on her face were a balm.

She wanted to stay here—right here—forever. Safe with Zach, who was good, and understood her somehow. A man who cared, and not just for show. She kept trying to convince herself it was just her dumb brain fooling herself again, but looking at that steady gaze she knew. She *knew* Zach was different.

And she was head over heels in love with a man she couldn't have.

But she kissed him anyway, fell to bed with him anyway, and let the sensations overwhelm her so she didn't think about anything except pleasure. Except finding release with this man who meant everything.

This man she'd have to say goodbye to, and soon.

But he kissed her, filled her, and for sparkling minutes of ecstasy she forgot everything except them.

ZACH WASN'T SURE he'd ever slept so soundly, or so long. He woke up feeling like a new man.

Of course, that might have been the sex.

Which really shouldn't have relaxed him considering it added quite a few complications to his nagging worry that Jordan's arrest was too easy. How could he tell the difference between what was true, and what his feelings for Lucy made him *want* to be true?

But facts were facts, right? There was evidence Jordan had done it. Why was he letting emotion sway the facts again? Didn't he know how that ended up?

He was almost grateful for the pounding on the door. If it didn't worry him. He slid out of bed as Lucy grumbled complaints.

Lucy. It was funny how easy it was to vacillate between the names. She seemed like both women to him, but somehow it seemed more…meaningful that he'd gone to bed with Lucy.

Possibly he was losing his mind.

He pulled on his pants and grabbed his

gun that he'd left in the nightstand. With the pounding continuing at increasing levels, he didn't have time to strap his holster on, so he simply held it behind his back as he made his way through the living room to the door.

He checked the security camera on his phone, but the man on the stoop wasn't familiar. He was about Zach's height, wearing jeans, an impeccably unwrinkled button-up shirt and a rather large cowboy hat.

Still, he was knocking. It could be information about Jordan. Zach eased the door open, weapon at the ready.

The man's cool blue eyes took in Zach's shirtless form and those eyes hardened.

"Can I help you?" Zach asked as he flipped the safety off behind his back.

"Vaughn!"

Zach glanced back at Lucy, who pulled the bright yellow robe she was wearing a little closer around her as she stepped forward.

Zach was glad he recognized the name as her brother's or the hot burn of jealousy at the pure delight in her tone might have had him acting stupidly and rashly.

"What are you doing here?" she asked, approaching them. She looked like she was about to lean in to hug her brother, but instead gripped her robe tighter. "I told you everything was fine."

Yeah, it wouldn't exactly be rocket science to figure out what they'd been doing together last night. And she certainly hadn't told him she'd contacted her brother.

"I came to take you home," Vaughn said, his voice cool and detached. But the words made Zach's blood run cold even as he set the gun back down on the counter.

"You didn't have to come collect me like I'm a sheep to be herded," Lucy countered. She glanced at Zach, but he couldn't read whatever was in her expression when she quickly looked away again.

"Maybe not," Vaughn countered. "But I thought Jordan being the suspect might hit you a little hard and you'd want—" he looked Zach up and down "—a friendly face."

"Uh, right. Well. Vaughn, this is Zach. I don't suppose you two have met, though you know of each other."

"Of each other, yes. Jaime spoke highly of you." After another moment of cold perusal, Vaughn offered his hand. "I was impressed by the detail in your reports."

Zach shook it. "Same goes. It's good to meet you," Zach offered, trying to sound businesslike despite the general lack of shirt, socks and shoes.

Vaughn did not return the sentiment, though it was hard to blame him. Zach hadn't had a normal brother-sister relationship with Hilly since they'd grown up apart, and she'd come into his life already connected to Cam, so there'd been no big-brother suspicion to be had.

But that didn't mean he couldn't understand Vaughn's. Especially considering Vaughn had arranged for Lucy's protection.

"Why don't you go get dressed?" Vaughn said to Lucy. He gave Zach a sharp smile. "Zach and I will chat."

Lucy rolled her eyes. "Yeah, you're a real chatterbox. But I'll go get dressed since I'll be more comfortable, and since I have no doubt Zach can stand up to the likes of you." She gave her brother a little poke, and then drifted her hand down Zach's arm as she sauntered away.

Zach thought he could probably handle her brother—Texas Ranger or not—but he didn't quite need her stirring the pot on the subject.

Especially when it gave him a quick few minutes alone with her brother, which meant, even though he still had his doubts, he had to tell Vaughn he didn't think this was over.

Somehow, he had to convince her brother that it wasn't Zach's heart doing the talking.

"I don't think she should go back home with you," he said when Lucy disappeared into the room, firmly and sure, but with absolutely no transition or finesse. He *could* have eased into it, but Lucy could also only take a few seconds to change. Time was of the essence.

Vaughn merely raised an eyebrow, reminding Zach a little uncomfortably of Lucy.

"I'm not saying Jordan isn't involved, but…" Zach knew he'd be shot down, but the incessant worry in his gut meant he had to say it. "There was evidence he's the murderer— I can't refute that. What concerns me are the loose ends. I'm not convinced this is it, or that Jordan's arrest means the danger to Lucy is over."

Vaughn studied him, and Zach braced himself for some kind of condescending lecture about being stupid.

It didn't come.

"I'm not, either," Vaughn said. When Zach could only stare at him, openmouthed, Vaughn continued. "Which is why I came out here. I didn't want her alone thinking she was safe, any more than I wanted to have to tell her she wasn't."

"Join the club," Zach muttered. He had

to tell her. *Had to*. And yet, she was just accepting her ex-husband was a murderer. How could he add the fact it didn't make Stacy or anyone else less potentially involved?

"Should I ask your intentions when it comes to my sister?" Vaughn asked with a wry twist of his lips.

"Why? Did we fall back in time a century? I'm pretty sure Lucy can handle my intentions." Not that he knew what they were, or why he suddenly wanted the curse to be true.

Vaughn didn't smile, but Zach didn't get the impression Vaughn was a particularly smiley guy. Still, his mouth loosened in what Zach would term *amusement*. Maybe.

"Lucy," Vaughn repeated as if surprised Zach was using her given name. "Well, that's new."

"Is it?"

Vaughn shrugged. "I don't make it a habit to poke into my sister's personal life, but she isn't keen on letting too many people call her by her real name."

It was funny how Vaughn said *real* and it didn't sit well with Zach. They were both real enough—Daisy and Lucy—they were both her. He shook his head. "So how do we break it to her?"

"I'd like to not. To protect her on the sly until we figure out the whole picture."

Zach snorted his derision, unable to stop himself.

"I said I'd *like* to, not that it would work." Vaughn sighed heavily and scrubbed a hand over his face. He didn't appear mussed by travel or beset by fatigue or worry, but that simple gesture told Zach he was all of those things. Sick to death worried about his sister's safety.

Vaughn gestured Zach to sit down on the couch, so Zach did so, Vaughn taking a seat next to him. "Quickest version you've got of the loose ends you think still exist?"

"Two main ones," Zach returned, keeping one eye on Lucy's bedroom door. "One, how Jordan had enough information to know Daisy was going to be with Stacy—which to me points to a potential connection with Stacy."

"What about other people in the office?"

"I laid a little bit of a trap. We gave information to Stacy and only Stacy—of course she might have slipped and told someone, but I'm willing to bet Stacy told Jordan, or someone who knows Jordan."

Vaughn shook his head. "That's going to hurt—worse than Jordan—if Stacy's involved."

"Yeah. And I'll be honest—the second

thread? I think there's someone else. Someone from her past, or maybe your father's. Someone who is using Jordan and Stacy and whoever else to exact some kind of...revenge."

"Why do you think that?"

"Patterns. Hunches. The way it's all played out."

Vaughn sighed. "You got notes?"

"You wouldn't believe the notes I have."

"I'll want some time to go over them." He glanced back at Lucy's still-closed door. "We don't have time."

"No. We don't. Look, why don't you let me tell her? That way she can be mad at me instead of her brother. We don't have to go into details. We can just say we're taking precautions until we're sure Jordan worked alone."

"How good of a liar are you, Zach?"

Zach's mouth quirked. "I've worked any number of undercover jobs for the FBI. How good of a liar do you think I am?"

"To her," Vaughn replied simply, which made Zach's stomach lurch. "Believe it or not, I've...been where you're standing. At least, if my assumptions are correct—and they usually are. Protecting someone can lead to a lot of strong feelings."

"I don't think we're going to appreciate you

warning me off. Grown adults. More important things at hand."

"The most important thing at hand is my
sister's safety. Which you've been in charge
of. Feelings—"

"Can complicate that. I'm well aware."

Vaughn gave him a look Zach couldn't
read, then shifted uncomfortably in his seat.
"Believe it or not, emotions aren't always the
enemy when it comes to keeping the people
you...care about safe."

"Not my experience, no offense."

"And yet in *mine*, I kept the woman safe,
married her and have two amazing kids with
her. So...you know. I guess it just depends."

Before Zach could say *anything* to that, because *marriage* and *kids* made his tongue stick
to the roof of his mouth, Vaughn switched
gears.

"Number one thing we should focus on?"

Zach forced himself to change gears, too.
"Jordan was arrested over an anonymous tip,
so someone out there knows something."

"It could be Stacy."

"It could be. No doubt."

But Zach was sure there was more, and that
he was running out of time to find it.

## Chapter Fifteen

That was how Lucy found her brother and her lover, heads bent together going over the details of her case. She couldn't hear what they were saying in their low tones, but it made her realize Jordan had never really mingled with her family or her friends.

He'd never sat next to Vaughn on a couch and discussed anything with this kind of serious back and forth.

Of course, Zach and Vaughn weren't exactly arguing the finer points of the Cowboys' defense or the Astros' pitching staff. They were discussing Jordan or the case or something about her. Keeping her safe, while she wandered around wondering how many people in her life had betrayed her.

The second they noticed her there, Vaughn loudly mentioned something about the home value of a place like this. Lucy shook her head. "All right. Let's cut the crap."

Zach looked back at her, picture-perfect innocence. She couldn't understand why his ability to put on and take off masks with such ease didn't scare her, but it didn't. It was a part of who he was, and so far he hadn't used it for any negative reasons against her.

"Crap?" he asked cheerfully. But he watched her, steady and concerned, and maybe that was why she couldn't get uneasy about him. He never pretended about his emotions toward her. Oh, he might bottle them up, but he didn't try to fake any.

She moved into the living room, fidgety and desperately trying to hide it by perusing the books laid out on the coffee table. She wanted to be steady and calm like them, but she never could really get there.

"Did they give Jordan a bond?" she asked, hoping to sound casual and unaffected. Last night Zach had explained to her that when it came to murder most judges denied bond, but in cities like Nashville it wasn't unheard of to simply set the bond high.

And she knew no matter how high a bond, Jordan wouldn't just be able to pay it, he'd be certain to.

"No bond. He'll stay put in jail until the trial," Zach returned, watching her in that eagle-eye way of his. She might not have minded that too much, but her brother was doing the same thing.

It brought home how much she'd kept Vaughn at arm's length over the years, and how much he would have been there for her if she'd let him. She couldn't blame his stoicism or disapproval, because it had been she who hadn't wanted to give anyone that piece of her.

She hadn't even given Jordan any pieces of herself. She'd weaved dreams and fantasies about their future, but she'd never let Jordan in on any of them. He'd been more like a statue to build her fantasies around than a person to build a life with.

He might have manipulated her and taken advantage of her vulnerabilities, but he wasn't exactly the whole reason their marriage had fallen apart. Any more than she could really truly believe he was the full reason Tom was dead, no matter how much she desperately wanted it to be that easy.

"He's going to have himself a hell of a lawyer," Lucy replied, trying not to sound grim or resigned, but perfectly reasonable instead. "Money buys a lot. He could be out in no time."

"I imagine you're right," Vaughn agreed, devoid of emotion one way or another.

She wanted to scowl at the both of them,

demand they *react* in some way, but they both looked at her. Concern and… Oh, she was stupid to think Zach was looking at her with love, but she'd already determined she was stupid, so why not just ride the wave?

"So when are we going to talk about the fact Jordan couldn't have known about the smoke bombs or to call to meet me without Stacy telling him?"

Vaughn sighed. "I'm sorry, Luce."

She tried to smile at Vaughn, though she knew it was weak at best. She perched herself on the arm of the couch on Zach's side. "I'm sorry, too, but…well, Jordan had a reason to hate me, I guess. Stacy didn't." No matter how many ways Lucy went back through the past few years, she couldn't even make up a reason.

Daisy Delaney could be prickly and difficult, but she'd always been those things with Stacy. Since those first days of stepping out of her father's shadow. Nothing about her behavior had changed. Except the addition of Jordan into her life and, in some ways, career. If this had happened while she was still married to Jordan, she might have been able to blame that, but she'd divorced him.

What reason did Stacy have to hate her now that she'd dropped the demanding weight around both their shoulders?

"I just can't understand why she'd want to hurt me. I know, I *know* there aren't other explanations for how Jordan got the info, but I can't understand it. That weighs on me."

"I've been pondering another angle," Zach said in that gentle way of his, which meant it would not be a gentle angle *at all*.

She saw the warning look Vaughn gave Zach and shook her head. She couldn't bury her head in the sand and let these two men handle things, though they would have gladly done it and it might be easier on her emotional well-being.

This whole time she'd been holding back, hoping things would right themselves. Hoping it would be taken care of by someone else, and it hadn't been. Oh, she'd thought about her past, who might hate her, but she hadn't tugged on old hurts or scars, because she'd thought surely all the people paid to keep her safe would figure it out.

But that just wasn't going to work. She needed to be present. She needed to revisit those scars so they could end this completely. Vaughn and Zach could only do so much— she was the real center of this problem— which meant she had to center herself in the solution.

Tom was dead. Jordan was in jail. She suspected one of her oldest, closest friends of being part of it.

Now was not the time to hide. It was time to be the woman in her songs—not just in name but in deed. The kind of woman who went after what she wanted and got it no matter the consequences, no matter what she had to sacrifice or lose.

She leveled Zach with an even stare. "What's the angle?"

"Your father."

She hadn't braced herself for that. The flinch that went through her had to be visible, and if only Zach had seen, that might have been okay, but Vaughn being here for this...

Vaughn hadn't had much of a relationship with Dad, and she knew that Dad's dying with no reconciliation weighed on him.

She stood back up and headed to the kitchen. She started the process of making coffee in the hopes that having something to do would ease her tightly wound insides. "Well, Stacy has a connection to Dad, sort of, as an assistant to Don. It's an awful long game for her to want to hurt me over something a dead guy did. Especially now after so many years of opportunity."

"I want to go back to the conversation we

had before the whole Jordan debacle. Your father's manager—Stacy's boss."

She stiffened again. She should have known Zach would come back to this, no matter how it didn't connect. "I don't see how this connects to Don."

"I don't, either, but we have the fact that he hurt you, which caused you to leave your father's fledgling label. After which, that label fell apart—if my research is correct."

"Don hurt you?" Vaughn demanded.

Lucy gave Zach a warning look not to say more. "It fell apart because Dad didn't know what he was doing. Excellent entertainer. Not so great on the business front. Everyone knew *he* was the reason for the failure, not me leaving."

"How did Don hurt you?" Vaughn demanded again.

"It was nothing," Lucy insisted. It bothered her to realize so many years later Vaughn would have supported her and protected her no matter what if she'd told him about the incident. But she'd known it would have come at the cost of the career she wanted...so she'd just kept quiet. Better to keep what she wanted and ignore the hurts, right?

"Lucy, you will tell me—"

"I don't need a big brother!" she shouted,

slamming the can of coffee against the counter. So much for being calm and collected—but who said calm ever got a woman anywhere? Maybe she needed to be *angry* and let it out. Maybe she needed to rage and act.

"I need this to be over," she said a little more evenly but with just as much emotion. "So look into Don Levinson, who is probably *dead*." She flung a hand toward Zach. "Look into anyone who might have hated my father. I'll give you every name I can think of. I just need this to *end*."

Zach stood, moving over to the kitchen. He didn't touch her, though she desperately wanted him to. Wanted that anchor to something solid and true, because no matter how she told herself to be strong, all her foundations were shifting under her. Zach seemed to be the one thing left that wouldn't.

"We all want it over, because we all want you safe," he said gravely.

She wanted to tell him she didn't know how to *deal* with that. Who had ever protected her? But that wasn't fair to Vaughn, who would have if she'd have let him. Because the real issue was, who had she ever *let* protect her?

*Zach.*

She didn't even have the good sense to question that because he stood there, handsome and sweet, and she'd never been so certain of Jordan. She'd convinced herself she was in love with Jordan, convinced herself to love him because of his act. But she'd never *felt* it wash over her as some irrefutable fact.

She'd had to work at loving Jordan and believing in that love. This thing inside her that waved over her whenever she looked at Zach was different, and it was real—no matter how little she understood that.

Zach wasn't an act. She'd *seen* him act. The real him was the man who'd made love to her last night.

She wished she could rewind time—stay right back there—where she didn't have to deal with loose ends or her brother.

But both had to be dealt with. Standing in this kitchen, looking at Zach, wishing this could be normal life without her safety in question—she realized for the first time in this whole nightmare year that at some point her life would be hers again.

She'd lived in the scary *now* for a year, most especially this past awful week. But it would have to end at some point and once it was over she'd have her life back. Completely. She'd be able to visit Vaughn and his family without worry. She'd be able to settle down somewhere and build whatever kind of life she wanted—including one with a partner, a real partner.

Maybe even in Wyoming. Maybe even with Zach. Why not? It was her fantasy life right now, so why not indulge in all those impossibilities?

"What about trying to ferret out the anonymous tip?" Vaughn asked, singularly focused on the task at hand. "Surely, the cops have some way of tracking it."

Zach turned back to his conversation with Vaughn, so Lucy focused on the coffee and the nice little fantasy of settling down in a ghost town where no one could find her if she didn't want them to. Zach could protect people and she could write music.

She was brought out of the reverie that eased some of that tension inside her by the vibrating of her phone in her pocket.

Lucy slipped the phone out and looked at the message. From Stacy.

She glanced at Vaughn and Zach, but they were deep in computers and papers and theories, so she opened the message.

911. Call back. No ears.

The *no ears* made her uneasy, but what could Stacy do over the phone? Maybe she was calling to warn her about something. Explain something. Hell, maybe she was calling to confess all.

She looked at the two men in her life again. They certainly didn't need her for whatever it was they were doing, and she wasn't so sure she needed them for this.

Part of her knew she should tell them about Stacy's text *before* she made the call, but they were handling everything else. Why couldn't she handle a simple phone call?

She opened her mouth to make her excuses, then realized neither one of them would come up for air for hours if she left them alone.

She eased her way into the hall. Then toward the back door. Slowly and as quietly as possible, she undid all three locks. She hadn't been out here, but Zach had mentioned a back porch she could use. She just hadn't had a reason to yet.

She stepped out onto it. It was less of a porch and more of a sunroom. The walls were made out of glass, glass she suspected was reinforced with whatever special security measures someone protecting people might use—if the giant keypad lock on the door to the outside was anything to go by.

Still, the day was sunny, and everything outside the glass was a vibrant, enticing green.

God, she was tired of being cooped up, of feeling like she had to be in someone else's presence for every second. She hadn't realized how much she missed just stepping outside and lifting her face to the sun.

Which meant this had to end and she had to talk to Stacy. She dialed Stacy's number, staring at the green outside, trying to breathe in the sunshine to offset the nausea roiling around inside her.

"Oh, thank God, Lucy. I don't know what's going on. Everything is so messed up. Jordan's in jail? What is happening?"

Stacy only ever called her Lucy outside work, those occasions they interacted as friends. Stacy had never had any trouble keeping both names straight. Was it because she was a two-faced backstabber?

"I don't know what's happening," Lucy replied flatly.

"Jordan's team is trying to lay the seeds that you've framed him."

Lucy snorted, lowering herself into a cushioned wicker chair and pulling her legs up under her. "The police didn't seem to think that was a possibility." She closed her eyes, trying to ignore the seed of fear and worry that Stacy had planted. God, would he succeed at that, too?

No one could prove she was trying to frame Jordan. Of course that didn't mean the tide of public opinion couldn't turn even further against her. That was what Jordan's team would try to do. Not just a wild, alcoholic cheater, but a murderer, too.

"I mean, Jordan's stupid enough to be set up," Stacy continued. "I'd certainly commend you for your creativity and for getting his big mouth out of the way."

"Are you accusing me of something, Stacy?" Lucy asked coldly, because an unforgiving chill had swept through her. Any conflict she had over not trusting Stacy was fading away with each statement. If Stacy was really worried about *her*, wouldn't this conversation go differently?

"No, God, of course not." Stacy sighed heavily into the receiver. "Everything is so messed up. So confusing. Can we meet for lunch?"

"Not without two bodyguards," Lucy retorted sharply.

"Two?" Stacy asked—the question one of confusion, or was it calculating the odds? Was it filing away information to use later?

It broke Lucy's heart to think Stacy was fishing. Broke Lucy's heart that she had to lie. "To start. You know how overprotective

Vaughn is. I swear he's hired half the country to look out for my well-being and investigate what on earth is really going on." She tried to make herself laugh casually, but couldn't muster the sound.

"You don't think Jordan did it?"

"All evidence points to yes, based on what I've heard, but you know, some people are more concerned for my safety than how much information I've got."

"You know, don't you?" Stacy said, her voice hushed and pained.

Lucy had to swallow at the lump in her throat. She waited for the confession, but Stacy didn't speak.

"What do I know, Stacy? Why don't you go ahead and tell it to me straight for once."

"God." Stacy's voice broke. "Don't hate me, Luce. It was an honest mistake. They all were."

An honest mistake. Tom was dead and Stacy had made an *honest mistake*. Lucy couldn't speak past the lump in her throat.

"Okay, okay. Just hear me out, okay? I know I'm the reason Jordan knew you were in town. I would have told you, but I didn't even realize it until someone told me you'd been at dinner together when he got arrested. Then I pieced it all together and—I'm sorry, okay?"

Lucy frowned. That wasn't exactly the grand confession she was expecting, but it was something. "You gave him the information about me coming here? Or going to Wyoming?"

"Here! Of course. You were totally safe in Wyoming," Stacy returned, and it was too hard to try and decide if she was an excellent liar or simply telling the truth.

"Truth be told, I don't understand why you came home when no one knew you were there."

"Because someone knew I was there, Stacy. I wasn't safe there. Someone found me. Now, what exactly did you tell Jordan? This time and before."

"Nothing before! How can you think that of me?" Stacy muttered a curse. "Listen, listen, okay? I hadn't talked to Jordan in months, but he called me not long after the smoke bomb. He was fishing, I knew he was, but he knew all the right buttons to push. I didn't mean to tell him. I was… He was being irritating, and I was trying to one-up him. I said I'd seen you at my office and you were *fine*. It wasn't until long after I'd hung up that I realized he was goading me and I was just dumb enough to bite."

It sounded plausible enough. God knew Jordan could manipulate. But how had someone found her in Wyoming? And why had Stacy pulled her in the opposite direction of Zach at the office?

Stacy wasn't copping to any of that, so what on Earth was this 911 emergency all about?

"Were you the anonymous tip?" Stacy asked after some beats of silence.

Lucy's blood chilled. "Pretty sure if I had any tips they wouldn't be anonymous, and I would have handed them over when I found Tom dead in my dressing room."

"Jesus," Stacy said, sounding truly sickened by the thought.

"Someone knew I was in Wyoming. You were the only person I told."

"You really think I'm behind this," Stacy said, sounding so shocked and hurt Lucy's own heart twisted in pain. But she had to be strong. Because manipulations were apparently the name of the game, and she'd fallen for too many.

"You were the only one outside my immediate family who knew where I was going," Lucy said, doubling down.

"I didn't tell anyone. Not a soul. Not even Cory. Cory…" There was a long pause.

"Don't try to pin this on Cory. What possible reason would she have for being involved in this?"

"It wasn't me, Luce. Whatever you think. I haven't done anything. I swear to God. I made a mistake in talking to Jordan, but…nothing else. How is this getting so out of hand?"

"What exactly is getting out of hand, Stacy? Because I'm lost."

Stacy swore again. "I might know… I have a bad feeling I know who's behind all this. Jordan told me something a long time ago that I never told you. I know I should have, but you were head over heels for him. If it didn't connect to some things with Cory lately, I might not have even remembered, but…"

"But what? What is it?"

The line was quiet except for Stacy's breathing. "Someone's here," Stacy whispered. "Oh, God, someone's in my house."

Fear bolted through Lucy sharply, and she forgot all of her suspicions at the sheer terror trembling through Stacy's voice.

"Stacy. Hang up. Call 911. Okay? Stacy?" Still shallow breathing. "Stacy!" Lucy yelled. "Hang up and call 911."

"Help m—"

The line clicked off.

# Chapter Sixteen

"Stacy's in trouble!"

Zach jumped to his feet, heart in his throat as Lucy ran into the living room.

"What?" he and Vaughn echoed in unison.

She waved her phone in both their faces. "I was talking to Stacy on the phone and—"

"Why the hell were you doing that?" Vaughn demanded. Which kept Zach from having to demand it.

"Zach," she said, turning to him, clearly thinking he'd be more reasonable than her brother. That wasn't the case, but he'd try to pretend. A sort of good-cop-bad-cop deal.

"She's at her house," Lucy said, panic in her voice and broad gestures. "She said someone was in her house and then the line went dead."

"Go back to the beginning," Zach said, trying to remain calm. "Explain everything."

She looked up at him helplessly. "There isn't time!"

"Lucy." He took her by the shoulders. "Just do it. Quickly, but from the beginning."

Lucy shook her head, still gripping the phone like it was a lifeline to Stacy. "She wanted me to call her. So I did, and she talked about Jordan being arrested, and said she accidentally told him about our meeting and me heading home."

Vaughn and Zach scoffed together.

"Look, I don't know. She seemed fishy and yet not and she was going to tell me something she thought I should know, then she said someone was in her house and her line went dead. She said *help*. Please." Blue eyes looked up at him, full of tears and fear. "Even if she's…part of this, she's in trouble."

Zach wasn't convinced that was true, but it was possible. It was also possible she was trying to lure Lucy to her house, and he'd use that if he could.

"Why didn't you tell us she was calling?" Zach asked, trying to be gentle.

"She wanted to talk privately," Lucy replied, sounding resigned. "But she was scared, Zach. That wasn't an act. I don't… It couldn't have been. I'm not saying it's on the up and up, but this is complicated and she's in *danger*."

Complicated was right.

"Call the cops," Zach instructed. He shook his head at Vaughn, who'd opened his mouth to speak. "Not you or me, her. She's the one who spoke with Stacy, so she's going to give them her account. You two stay put. But call the cops and tell them everything you remember about the phone call."

"You don't know that she's telling the truth," Vaughn said firmly.

"No, but I don't know that she's not," Zach returned, moving for his gun, his holster, keys, wallet. "If this is some sort of plot to get to Lucy, she'll be here, protected by you and out of harm's way. If it's not, then I get close enough to see what she might be planning. I'll need her address."

"Wait, you're not…going," Lucy said incredulously.

"If she's in trouble, I'm going to help," Zach said, weapon already strapped to his body. "And if she's trying to lure you, I want to be there to figure out why."

"But the cops—"

"I want them to check it out, but I want to get there first in case something is off. The more information I can gather, the better chance we have of putting this away for good."

"But if it's a lure, it could be dangerous. You could be hurt."

"Not if you call the cops." He didn't like Lucy being out of his sight right now, but they were both going to have to deal with their worry. Vaughn would protect her. He was more than capable. "Make sure you tell the cops I'll be there and give my description and that I'll be happy to verify and ID who I am so they don't mix me up with anyone else."

He leaned forward to kiss her goodbye— just on the off chance this was dangerous and things went south—but the presence of her brother gave him pause.

Screw it. He kissed her. Hard. "Stay put. I mean it. Both of you." He didn't need to worry about Vaughn keeping an eye on her. There was no doubt in Zach's mind Vaughn would lay down his own life to save his sister's, just like Zach would do.

So Zach would go, no matter how much uncertainty plagued him. Because this didn't add up and if it was a lead, he'd darn well take it. "Text me the address."

By the time he was in the rental car, Stacy's address was plugged into his navigation system and he was on his way.

He wished he had more time to plan, but if Lucy sincerely thought Stacy was in trouble there wasn't time for plans. He had to act. Stacy might be involved, like Jordan, and about to be hurt to protect a killer's true identity. Stacy could be luring Lucy to her, or trying to get her alone.

Endless possibilities. So he had to be ready for anything.

He beat the cops to her house, which wasn't too far from the farmhouse. That certainly gave him some pause, but he quickly got out of the car and began moving toward the house.

It was quiet. Stacy didn't have the same amount of property as the place they'd been staying, but it was still secluded from the neighbors by a pristine lawn and thick trees around the perimeter.

Zach glanced into the garage through the windows. There was a car parked inside the tidy building. If someone was here, there was no evidence of a vehicle besides Stacy's own.

He didn't want Stacy to be guilty for Lucy's sake, but believing things for Lucy's sake was bound to get people hurt. He'd already let his emotions get too involved here even after promising himself not to.

That was... Well, it had happened. He couldn't change it.

So he'd have to do better for Lucy than he'd done for Ethan. Neither Lucy nor her brother were getting hurt on his watch, so he'd follow this path wherever it led.

He moved to the front door, glanced around the quiet lawn. Nothing and no one, as far as he could tell.

Carefully, he tried the knob. Locked. He looked around again, hoping for police backup, but still no sign of cops or sounds of sirens.

He'd have to move around the house, looking in what windows he could. Then if there was still nothing—and no cops—he'd simply have to break in and hope for the best.

He moved stealthily around the house, peeking in windows and seeing nothing—no people, no signs of struggle, just a perfectly neat but lived-in-looking house.

Until he got to the back porch. There were two big French doors that led into a dining room and kitchen area.

The bolt of shock at what he saw stopped him in his tracks. Stacy was sitting in the middle of the kitchen—tied to a chair. She had duct tape around her mouth. He could see her profile, and her eyes were wide and terrified.

There didn't appear to be anyone around her—though he could only see part of the kitchen and dining room from his vantage point. He looked around the expansive backyard. No one.

It could be a trap—the way his heart beat

hard against his chest warned him that this could all end very, very badly for him.

But a woman was tied up in a kitchen and he was armed. The least he could do was try to help her.

He could tell the doors weren't fully latched—likely where whoever was in there had gotten in—so he began to slowly move forward, watching every inch of the backyard for a flash of movement.

Every last hunch inside him screamed *trap*, but he couldn't ignore the trickle of blood that started at Stacy's temple and slid down the side of her face and neck.

It was possible she'd done it to herself, possible she was *this* good of an actor, but he couldn't be sure.

Carefully, making as little noise as possible, Zach inched forward. He kept his gaze alert and his movements careful, gun at the ready. He moved up to the door and waited for some kind of movement.

When he reached forward and gave the door a slight nudge, Stacy's head whipped around. Her eyes went wide. Zach could only hope she recognized him as he stepped forward.

She didn't fidget or try to speak past the tape. She just watched him as she breathed heavily through her nose. Slowly, she moved her hand. Though her arms were tied to her sides and the chair, she lifted one finger and pointed upstairs.

At least, that was what he hoped she was pointing at. He moved closer and closer, studying the way she was tied. It would be best to free her arms and legs first, so she could run if need be, but he needed more information first. So the tape had to go.

"Brace yourself, okay?" he whispered, tapping the edge of the tape. "And try not to make a sound."

She nodded, tears trickling down her cheeks. Feeling awful, Zach pulled the tape from her mouth.

She gasped in pain, but she didn't make any extra noise.

"How many are there?" he asked, immediately crouching to untie the rope bonds.

"Just one. Just one. I don't know who he is. I don't know what's going on." She started crying in earnest, and Zach winced at the noise. "He's upstairs. He's looking for something, but I don't know what."

"That's fine. It's all going to be okay." He got the ropes off her and helped her to her feet. "Run outside. The police will be here soon. I'm going to stay right here and make sure he doesn't leave, so you just make sure to tell the police there are two of us in here—and one of us means them no harm." Hopefully, between Stacy's recount and Lucy's call giving his description, he'd avoid accidentally entangling with police.

"What are you going to do?" Stacy whispered, rubbing her arms where the rope had been.

"I'm going to find out what's going on once and for all. You run. Now."

She nodded tremulously, but then she eased out of the back door and left in a dead run.

Zach took a breath and then began to move. He wished he knew the layout of Stacy's house, but he could at least hear someone upstairs. As long as he did, he knew the perpetrator was up there and not on the same level as him.

Zach just needed to find him, get him to talk and then let the police do whatever they had to do.

Easy, right?

He eased closer to the staircase, weapon drawn and ready. Here he couldn't hear the footsteps as well as he'd been able to in the dining area.

Still, he moved slowly and as silently as possible. As he went up the stairs, some of his old FBI training took over—the way his body would cool, tense and let go of the wild fear. Focused on the job—on the end result, and the rest of the chips would fall where they fell.

Doing what he came to do was the most important thing.

When he crested the top, he leaned forward and looked around. There weren't any hallways, just a circle of an area—with four rooms around him.

All four doors were open, but only slightly ajar. If he started to move forward, he'd be able to get a glimpse into them, but he wouldn't be able to do anything else without drawing attention to himself.

Not ideal, but it could be worse, so he started forward. The first room didn't have anyone in it that he could see. Neither did the second room. As he approached the third, his foot landed on a floorboard that made a creak as loud as a bomb.

Immediately, the third door burst open and a gun went off. Zach felt the searing burn of metal hitting flesh, stumbled to his hands and knees and swore, then rolled forward to knock the shooter off his feet.

His arm throbbed, but not enough to be anything more than a flesh wound. The gunman let out a howl of pain as he crashed into the dresser. Violent cursing and threats spewed from the man, but it was drowned out by the thundering of feet and shouted orders to drop their weapons and stay down.

Zach winced at the searing ache in his arm, but praised the timing of the police. The man he'd knocked into wasn't taller than Zach, but he was built like a Mack truck. Zach could take on a bigger man, but in this tiny room he would have been beat to hell in the process, no doubt.

Once the cops verified who he was and cleared him to get up, he moved toward the man he didn't recognize being handcuffed.

"Who do you work for?" Zach demanded.

"We'll handle the questioning, Mr. Simmons."

Zach leveled the officer pushing him back with a scathing look. Zach kept trying to push forward, but the one cop kept pushing him back while two others arrested the thrashing man on the ground.

Zach cursed. Demanded answers. Got nothing but a brick wall of blank-faced cops as they hauled the assailant down the stairs.

The last cop eyed him, nodded toward his arm. "There's an ambulance outside."

Zach looked down. Blood was trickling down his arm and onto the white carpet. He blinked at the tiny pool of blood. For a second he felt a little light-headed, but then he shook it off.

"I'm fine." He had to find some answers before this escalated any further. "I need answers. I need—"

"Nasty gash on his head. He'll be transported to the hospital, and then we'll take him in for questioning. I'd suggest calling one of our detectives tomorrow to get an update on the situation."

Tomorrow. An *update*? He didn't have time to wait until tomorrow. "Where's the woman?" Zach asked.

"What woman?"

Zach's entire body went cold, his gut sinking with dread. "The one who ran out of here a good ten minutes ago."

The cop's eyebrows drew together, and he pulled his shoulder radio to his mouth and muttered a few things into it. After a few seconds of static and responses, the cop shrugged. "No one saw a woman."

*Hell.* "There was a woman here, tied up and mouth taped." He went through the whole event, gave Stacy's name and description, and then rushed back to the farmhouse, trying to determine what on earth Stacy had been trying to pull. She'd been hurt, but now she was missing.

What was going on? He couldn't figure it out for the life of him, but one thing he knew for sure.

He had to get back to Lucy and make sure she was okay.

LUCY PACED IRRITABLY. "It's taking too long. Why hasn't he called? Or come back? What if he's hurt and we're just sitting here—"

"If the police are questioning him, it'll take a while," Vaughn replied calmly. "These things take time, and unfortunately going half-cocked is likely what Stacy wanted. We have to stay put and wait and trust the police to do their jobs."

"Why would they question Zach?"

"Because they have to piece together what happened. If Zach sees anything over there, he'll need to explain. Maybe he's giving them more details on the case. You just don't know, and you can't read into the time that passes. Sit. Relax."

She snorted. "How can I relax when… when…" She plopped down on the couch next to Vaughn. She'd never told her brother anything about her personal life, and vice versa, but she didn't have anywhere else to put all this *stuff* roiling around inside her.

"I'm in love with him."

Vaughn leveled her with a bland gaze. "Gee. You don't say."

She frowned at him. She thought she'd get a lecture…one that would give her a reason to be mad and rage instead of be sad or worried.

Vaughn offered no such lecture and, in fact, seemed wholly unsurprised and unconcerned.

"You're okay with that?"

"Not *okay* exactly, but I know a thing or two about…falling in love under uncomfortable circumstances."

"He might not be in love with me," Lucy replied petulantly, because she wanted to be petulant about something if she couldn't be mad.

"Lucy, please. He's so head over heels even I can't be big-brother outraged over it. I might not be particularly comfortable with emotion, but I certainly recognize head-over-heels stupid love when I see it."

"It's just the pressure. He feels guilty. He had this thing go wrong when he was in the FBI, and… You don't fall in love over the course of a few days. It's adrenaline and stuff."

Vaughn didn't even have the decency to look away from the computer screen he was still doing research on. "I'll be sure to let Nat know the only reason I fell in love with her was *adrenaline and stuff.*"

"That's not the same."

This time he did look at her, but only to give her his patented condescending older-brother look. "How exactly?"

She didn't have a good answer, so she was more than happy that her phone trilling interrupted the question. She stood and answered without even looking at the caller ID. "Zach?"

"Lucy. No. No, it's me."

"Stacy?" She grabbed Vaughn's arm as he shot to his feet next to her. She was scared to death Stacy was calling to tell her Zach had been hurt or worse.

"What's happening? What is *happening*? I'm so scared. God."

"Stacy. Where are you? Where's Zach?" Lucy demanded through a tight throat.

Vaughn ripped the phone out of her hands. She thought he was going to talk to Stacy himself, demand answers, but he only put the call on speaker.

"He saved me," Stacy was saying over and over again. "He saved me, but… Lucy." Stacy was breathing hard, and the connection was spotty. "Listen to me."

The line cut in and out. "Stacy. Stacy. Stop…running? Or whatever you're doing. Stay in one place. I'm losing you."

"I'm so scared. Zach told me to run, so I ran and now… I don't know where I am. I ran into the trees and now… God, I'm so lost. I know I should have waited for the police, but I was so scared."

She started crying and Lucy's heart twisted, some awful mix of compassion and suspicion. What if this was another fake thing? "Stacy, tell me what's going on."

"I don't know. I don't understand it, but I think… Lucy, Jordan is Don Levinson's grand-nephew."

"What?" Daisy asked incredulously. The only reason she didn't lose her balance was because Vaughn held her up.

"Yes. God. He told me at some party eons ago. I didn't think much of it. You and I had already had a fight about Jordan and I didn't want to make you madder at me over Jordan. But then I mostly forgot about all that. He never brought it up again, and I never saw the old bastard. But I think Cory is involved, Lucy. I really do. I didn't tell anyone you'd been to Wyoming. Not a *soul*. But Cory could have been listening. It's the only possibility."

Lucy shared a look with Vaughn. He didn't look convinced, but Jordan was related to *Don*? Why would Don want to hurt her after all this time? How did it all connect?

"Okay. Okay. You just stay put," Lucy instructed. They needed her safe and coherent to figure out if her story made any sense. "I'm going to come find you."

Before Vaughn could mount his argument, Stacy gave one. "No, Lucy. You can't. Whoever was in my house... I didn't recognize him or know him. Whoever wants to hurt you is still out there, pulling strings."

Which was when they heard a car squeal to a stop in front of the farmhouse.

## Chapter Seventeen

Zach screeched to a stop in front of the farm-house. He all but leaped out of the car and ran for the door. Stacy missing, the cops not having seen her at all, made every terrible scenario run through his head.

Stacy had already beaten him here. The whole thing had been a ruse to find out the location of the farmhouse. It was too late and Lucy was—

He stopped on the porch on a dime. What if he'd fallen for it, and led Stacy—or who-ever—here right *now*? Stacy was a plant, but not the kind he'd expected. Not trying to lead Lucy to an ambush at her place, but a way to find Lucy at hers.

He turned, looked around the yard, but there was no sign of anyone that he could see. If someone had followed him, they were still far enough away that he could get to Lucy and keep her safe.

Unless they were already here. He jumped forward and shoved his key into the lock. He'd get to Lucy first. Move them out fast. Then they could figure it out, but first they had to be away from any place that could be dangerous and breeched.

The sound of an explosion shuddered through the air in perfect timing with a blast of pain in his thigh. He staggered forward, the door opening as he did so. He crashed to the ground of the entryway, just barely recognizing the scream as Lucy's.

Lucy. Who he had to keep safe, no matter how his vision dimmed or the pain screamed through him. This wound was worse than his arm, but it wasn't fatal. Probably.

Even if it was, he'd do whatever it took to make sure nothing fatal touched Lucy.

Zach managed to scoot back and kick the door closed, but it wasn't fast enough. Before Vaughn could jump on the lock, it was being flung back open and Vaughn got knocked into the coffee table, which broke and splintered under his weight.

Two men stepped inside, one holding a gun, and one looking very, very smug. They shut the door behind them.

Zach didn't know why he was surprised. He'd known, hadn't he?

Emotion got people hurt and killed. He'd let his worry over Lucy cloud his thoughts, and now they'd all pay for it.

"WELL, LOOK AT YOU, Daisy girl. All grown."

Lucy's stomach pitched. The years had not been kind to Don Levinson, and yet that smarmy smile of his was exactly the same and still reminded her of things she'd tried long and hard to forget.

That smile made her remember all too clearly a young girl who'd thought her father would protect her and been wholly, utterly disillusioned.

But Dad was dead, and Don very much wasn't. Old, yes, but not dead, and certainly no less evil than he'd been all those years ago trying to take advantage of young women.

Vaughn sat in the wreckage of the coffee table. Zach lay on the ground, a concerning amount of blood pooling around his leg. Both were armed, but neither reached for their weapon. She supposed they wouldn't as long as Don's little buddy there had a very big and scary-looking gun pointed in her direction.

"I'm very disappointed in you, sweetheart. Your father always told me how smart you were, and yet you never once suspected your old pal Don. You didn't suspect that moron you married until it was too late."

Lucy didn't say anything. She barely let the words register, because she had to think. She had to survive this and get Zach and Vaughn out of this horrible mess.

"Don't worry. You're not half as disappointing as *him*," Don continued. "The time and effort I poured into that boy, and he's still dumb as a post. A bit of a coward, too. If I'd had my way, he would have killed you slowly and quietly when you were married, but *no*."

Killed her. Don and Jordan had plotted to kill her.

"He thought he'd use your fame instead of my know-how. Thought you being a wreck would sell him better than you being dead. Well, look where he is now. Like I said, dumb as a post."

"Yeah, I suppose we both were," Lucy replied, trying not to let the wave of nauseous regret fell her. Zach was bleeding. Vaughn would die to protect her and leave his family without a husband and father.

She couldn't—wouldn't—let that happen.

"What on earth do you have against me, Don?" Lucy asked, trying to sound bored and unaffected.

Don laughed. "Against *you*. Against *you*?

As if you don't know. Your father told me what you did."

"Told him you were a dangerous pervert who couldn't keep his hands off teenage girls?"

"If you hadn't gone crying to him, pretending like you hadn't wanted my hands on you, do you know what I would have? He cut me out of his estate, and out of all I'd invested in *you*. So I had to bow and scrape and pay off my debts. The things I had to endure because I didn't get that money, all because you were a lying whore. Well, my hands'll be on you now."

Zach and Vaughn made almost identical sounds of outrage, and Don smiled down at them. "Don't worry," he said cheerfully. "It won't bother you any. You'll both be dead." His gaze went back to Daisy. "And boy, will the press eat this up. I'll have to figure out how I'm going to play it first. You'd think I'd know, with all the planning that's gone into it, but sometimes I do like to wing it. Murder-suicide? Or do I just frame you? So many options. But at least I finally realized I'd have to do it myself. The younger generation just doesn't have the chutzpa to get things done."

He turned to the other man. "Leave the one on the floor." He nudged Zach with his boot.

Zach didn't so much as move or groan. Lucy tried not to panic that he'd lost consciousness. "He'll bleed out if he hasn't already." Don then studied Vaughn.

Lucy had to do something. Save her brother. Save Zach. But how? If someone was willing to kill like this, what kind of reasoning would work?

"You want money?" she demanded.

"I want *revenge*, little girl. I was supposed to have a piece of your pie, but your father held your lying story over me for years. Made me jump through all those hoops and then not even a *cent* of his estate? Which should have been rightfully left to me for all I'd done to make him a star, if you hadn't come along."

"I never lied. You grabbed me."

"You begged for it."

"You're delusional. And insane, I think, to have spent your life so obsessed with me—"

"Shoot her," Don ordered of the man with the gun. Then he held up a hand, before Vaughn could lunge to her rescue, and sighed dramatically. "No. That's rash. I want my fun with her first. And yours, as well," he said, nodding toward the man with the gun, who smiled.

Lucy hoped she didn't go gray, because it felt as though the very blood leaked out of her. But she needed to keep Don talking, not acting. She had to make him feel…superior. Anger would make him act, but condescension would keep his diatribes going.

"You were never supposed to have a piece of my career. My career was always separate from Dad's."

Don tipped his head back and laughed, all too heartily. Lucy noted Zach's lifeless body. Vaughn's hesitant, slow and deliberate move for his hand to get closer and closer to his weapon without drawing attention.

She needed a scene. Not just from Don, but from everyone to get the man with the gun's attention.

"You were always meant to be your daddy's pawn. Problem was you got too many ideas, and that uppity assistant of mine fed them. And if your father had listened to me, you both would have been taken down a peg. But he let you go instead. Costing me millions. *Millions.*"

The rage was starting to seep back in and Lucy racked her brain for a way to fix this. Save them. But Don just kept going, eyes gleaming with vicious rage, spittle forming at the corners of his mouth.

And all the while the man with the gun had the barrel pointed right at Lucy's heart.

"Then he didn't even have the intelligence to be sorry. Every time, every single time I had a better idea for your father's career, one he didn't agree with, what did he say to me? *I guess Daisy going to the police wouldn't be such a good thing for* your *career, would it, Don?*"

"That sounds like a problem between you and my father," Lucy managed, though her throat was tight with fear and pain.

"A problem I solved." He grinned and Lucy's knees nearly gave out.

"You killed him?" she rasped.

Don shrugged, but his smile was sharp. "Not so much. Supply him enough drugs and he killed himself." But his smile turned into a sneer. "Then I started getting your notes."

"I never sent you any notes, Don. I'd forgotten you even existed. That's why I didn't suspect you were behind this, because you're so far beneath me and behind me I didn't give you a second thought." Notes. Notes. As if this wasn't complicated enough, someone had been sending him notes in her name?

"Sure, little girl. Sure."

"Maybe Jordan isn't as stupid as you thought," Lucy shot out. "He knew, you know. About what you did to me." It was a flat-out lie. The only person she'd ever told aside from Stacy was Zach.

Oh, God, it all circled back to Stacy, didn't it?

But she couldn't get caught up on that. She couldn't let the tears that threatened, fall. She couldn't give in to panic or fear, because Zach was a lifeless, bleeding form on the floor and she had to save him.

Jordan was safe in jail. If she implicated him, if she got Don to believe it…well, he'd kill them all anyway, but maybe it would make him unbalanced for a few minutes.

Don narrowed his eyes at her. "I don't believe it."

"I didn't send you notes, Don. You would have been one of the top suspects if I had. It had to be Jordan. Unless you told someone else about it."

"Or your father did." He shook his head. "It doesn't matter. Result is still the same. This guy is dead." He pointed at Zach. Then he pointed at Vaughn. "That guy is going to be. And we're going to have our fun before you are, too."

No. That was not how this was going to go down, and the best way to get out of a sticky situation with a man who thought he was in charge was always, *always* act the over-wrought female.

"Dead?" she moaned. "He's dead?" She made a choking, sobbing noise and flung herself on Zach's body.

She'd hoped it would be enough of an opening Vaughn would shoot, but Don just grumbled something about women. So Lucy sobbed as loudly as she could, moving her hand, discreetly trying to get to Zach's gun without anyone noticing.

It wasn't hard to keep crying when he didn't move. But he was breathing. Unless it was just the movement of her own body making his chest seem as though it was moving up and down. She was almost to his gun when she felt him twitch under her just a little.

She gave herself one second to just press her cheek to his chest and breathe in some relief. He was alive but he desperately needed help. She'd give it. Get his gun and—

"Scream," Zach whispered through bloodless lips, but he was breathing and talking, so she didn't wait around for anything else. She did exactly what he said.

LUCY'S SCREAM SHATTERED through the air and though it hurt like hell, Zach whipped his gun out of his holster and shot the man with the gun—who'd been so intent on Vaughn's lunge he hadn't seen Zach move, and with Lucy sheltering his arm from Don, the old man hadn't been able to warn him.

Vaughn tackled Don to the floor amidst shouts and threats.

Zach tried to get to his feet, but leveling the gun had taken all his energy and focus. His vision wavered, and he wasn't all that certain he could feel his legs. There was only pain and a fog that he kept trying to fight.

It was starting to win.

"Get some pressure on the wound," he thought he heard Vaughn shout. Was Lucy hurt? No, she hadn't been—had she?

Zach had shot the right guy, and Vaughn had taken care of the rest. Lucy was safe. He relaxed a little into the fog, except there were still so many unanswered questions.

"Loose ends," Zach muttered.

Gentle hands were on his face. "Only a few. You just stay with me so we can figure them out, all right?"

"Lucy."

"That's right. That's right." There was a catch in her throat and even though he could only see black, he knew she was crying. But she was here and safe and that was what mattered.

He hissed out a breath, eyes opening as pain

shot through his leg. Pressure, he supposed, but it hurt too much to hold on to consciousness. He tried not to slide away while Lucy whispered things in his ears.

"You're okay, baby. I promise."

Something floated around in his head, a feeling he had to tell her. But the words didn't form. Yet, it was imperative. He had to tell her so she knew, but every time he tried to speak it all floated away.

"Zach, stay with me. We need you here."

"I'm here." But he wasn't. He kept losing hold on himself, on her.

There was noise, and he was being jostled. Lucy faded away, and so did he, but words floated with him.

"I love you, Zach. I love you. So you just hold on to that or I'm going to be really pissed."

Those were the words he'd meant to find— *I love you, I love you*—if only he could manage to say them back.

## Chapter Eighteen

Everyone insisted she go to the police station. Vaughn was with her, but no one was with Zach. No matter what Vaughn said about him being in surgery and her not being able to be with him anyway, she could only think about him being alone.

The detective who sat at the desk across from them looked frazzled, which wasn't exactly comforting. "It doesn't add up. Let's go over it again."

"She's gone over it enough," Vaughn said firmly. "You have to find Stacy Vine. She'll fill in some of these missing pieces."

"Yes, I know. We're searching for her. We've got a team combing the woods as Ms. Delaney described to us from their phone call, and we've got someone watching her office as well as her car." The detective sighed, and then tapped a few things on his computer. "We've got someone searching Don Levinson's place of residence for evidence of these letters allegedly from you. Also, obviously, any evidence pertaining to the murder of Tom Perelli, the break-in at Stacy Vine's house or any connection to the three hired men that have been involved in attacks on Ms. Delaney."

"That's all well and good, but it isn't answers."

"Answers take time, Ranger Cooper," the detective returned, losing some of his control as irritation snaked into his tone.

Lucy couldn't blame him. It seemed no matter how they dug, no one could find all the answers. And her being here wasn't changing that, so she had to go to the hospital.

Before she could thank him for his time, make her excuses to go to the hospital, a knock sounded at the door to the detective's office.

Lucy didn't know how long they'd been sitting here, but it felt interminable.

And then Cory, Stacy's assistant, was being walked in. Handcuffed.

"Cory?"

"I didn't do anything! I didn't do a *thing*." But Lucy's stomach sank as she noticed anger more than fear in the depths of Cory's eyes. The same kind of anger that had been in Don's.

"She was found in Ms. Vine's house. An officer found her placing these in Ms. Vine's belongings." The officer held out a ziplock bag and the detective studied them. Then he turned them to Lucy.

"Is this your handwriting, Ms. Delaney?"

Lucy studied the words. *You spineless lowlife, you owe me for what you did. I'm going to make you pay worse than my father did.*

"No. Not my handwriting and I didn't write those."

Cory started screaming, blaming Don and Lucy and Stacy at equal turns, not making much sense in the process. The officer who'd led her in led her back out.

Lucy closed her eyes against the roil of nausea. She felt…sorry for the girl, almost. It was too easy to be manipulated by powerful men who'd always trusted their own influence, when you always questioned your own.

Vaughn's arm came around her and she leaned into it.

Hours passed as she sat in the awful police station. They finally found Stacy, and Lucy didn't know how to repair the damage of the past few days. But the police seemed to believe Stacy was innocent—that Cory's connection to Don had led her to ferret out information and supply Don with it.

Cory, a woman Don had groomed from the time she'd moved to Nashville with a dream of becoming a country music star. He'd pushed her into getting a job for Stacy, pumped her for information about Daisy over the years. Don had used that information to supply bits and pieces to Jordan. Who had, in the end, not used it quite the way Don had wanted.

But Don also hadn't helped Cory the way she'd expected, so Cory had begun using the information *she* knew about Don against him—writing threatening letters supposedly from Daisy.

Which had finally forced Don to act, instead of just stew. Especially when Daisy had filed for divorce from Jordan.

Jordan, who hadn't been released from jail yet, but it was looking like he would be.

Vaughn was insisting the detectives look into the legality of him getting off scot-free when he'd known Don had wanted her dead, but Lucy didn't care about that.

"I just want to see Zach. And then I want…" She wanted to go home. Only she didn't have one.

"We'll take it one step at a time, and I'll be here for every step. Whether you want me to be or not. That's a promise for the rest of your life."

Lucy smiled, but she also cried. And Vaughn held her through the tears, no matter how uncomfortable he was. He always would have, but now she was promising herself to always let him.

ZACH WOKE UP, groggy and gray. Pain snaked through a void of numbness. He didn't know where he was or why he was here, except he was clearly hurt.

When he managed to open his eyes, blue ones stared right back at him. Something inside him eased. She was all right.

"Your mother will be so upset with me. I just convinced her to go back to her hotel and get some sleep and here you are waking up."

"Aw, hell. My mother?" Zach grumbled, his voice raw.

Lucy took his hand in hers. "She likes me, don't worry. Cam and Hilly wanted to come, too, but I think your mother told them to stay put so they could take shifts."

"Cam's probably pretty pissed I went dark."

"Cam will probably forgive the man who's been shot twice."

He looked at her, really looked, as he came back to himself. He didn't remember much of what had happened, and based on the itchy

and uncomfortable scruff on his face, he'd
been out for a while.

But he remembered her saying she loved
him, like one bright, shining beacon in the
middle of foggy dark.

"Supposed to be a Delaney that gets shot,"
he managed to say, earning one of her patented raised eyebrow looks that made the love
sweep through him so hard, so fast, he'd never
question anyone's view on meant-to-be again.

"You see, back in Bent, there's a feud," he
said over the wave of pain.

"You've been holding another good story
from me?"

A story she'd love. A story that didn't scare
him anymore. Because when it came to love,
there were lots of things to worry about, but
none to be scared of. "Carsons and Delaneys.
They don't like each other. My mother was a
Carson. Your grandmother was a Delaney."

"Are we Romeo and Juliet, Zach?"

"No, because I'm willing to die for you,
Lucy, but I'm not willing to kill myself over
you. Besides, the past year or so it's been
something of a…hate to love deal. Carsons
and Delaneys kept pairing off. Until I was the
only one left."

"So we're meant to be."

"I've never believed in meant-to-be," Zach

replied, holding her hand in his. She was looking worse for the wear herself, worrying over him. So many loose ends, but she was here and okay, and he was here and okay, so the most important loose end was love. "But I believe we got thrown into each other's life for a chance at something I never really thought I'd have."

"A country duo?"

"You're on quite the comedic roll, aren't you?"

"If I don't laugh I might break down and cry, and I've cried myself dry. So, I'd rather laugh, if you don't mind."

"I don't mind. I don't mind anything, if you're here. I love you, Lucy."

She swallowed, eyes shining. "I want it to go down on the record I was brave enough to say it first."

"Or at least smart enough to realize it first. I needed to get shot. Twice."

"You're just more stubborn than me."

"Ha!" The scoffing laugh hurt and he winced.

"I need to call the nurse in."

"No, not just yet. Come here."

She scooted closer and brushed a gentle kiss across his cheekbone.

"Going to come visit me? A lot?"

"Nah."

The pain of getting shot had nothing on the simple slice of horror that cut through him, until he noted she was smiling and leaning forward.

"I'd rather come home with you instead. I've got some ideas for your little ghost town."

Relief coursed through him like a river. "Do you now?"

"I'll still make music, and tour, and you'll work with Cam and keep people safe even if it puts you in danger. Because my songs and your protection is who we are."

"Yes, it is."

"But I want to build a life with you where I can come home and be Lucy Cooper when Daisy Delaney wears me out."

"I want that, too." God. More than he could express.

"So you'll have to heal up quick. Nashville's got too many prying eyes, and one too many men named Jordan Jones."

"All right. I'm ready. Tell me the whole thing."

He fell asleep halfway through her explanation of Don's plans, Cory's role, Jordan's half guilt and Stacy's innocence. It took him another few days to make it through the whole story, and more time after that to get out of the hospital, and then back onto a plane to Wyoming.

With Lucy Cooper at his side. Just where she belonged.

# Epilogue

Zach Simmons was not a sentimental man, or so he'd thought. The sight of his mother carefully assisting Hilly with her wedding dress outside the church that had been restored in Hope Town—the name Lucy had come up with for their little ghost town—shifted something inside him.

Hilly made a beautiful bride, and their mother's elegant form standing next to her, openly crying, made his heart swell—a mix of sweet and bitter. He knew Mom was missing Dad, but also happy for Hilly, who'd been through so much and deserved this pretty wedding.

"Mom, you're supposed to go take your seat."

She nodded, dabbing at her eyes. She gave him a quick hug, beaming at him.

"You're looking good," she offered before slipping out of the room.

*Good* was probably a tiny exaggeration. He still had a ways to go on his recovery for his leg, but even Lucy had gotten to a place where she didn't get irritated about his jokes over it. After all, only Delaneys got shot in their pursuit of happily-ever-after. He'd bucked tradition—being the best of the Carsons and all that.

"You look beautiful," he said to Hilly once Mom had gone.

Hilly shook her head. "Don't say nice things to me. I'm trying not to cry until I see Cam. Is he nervous?"

"Cool as a cucumber." Which had been true on the surface, but his obsessive attention to detail at the church had been a sure giveaway Cam wasn't as calm as he pretended.

Lucy had called it cute. Zach had scoffed at her.

Zach offered an arm and then walked out of the small room Hilly had gotten ready in. They moved into the lobby of the church. Hilly and Cam had foregone bridesmaids and groomsmen since they had so many family members they would want to stand up with them. They'd said a church full of people they loved was enough—and that was exactly what they were getting.

So Zach waited for the signal—a text from

Jen—and when it came, he opened the door. He led Hilly down the aisle.

There were people missing from the wedding. Their father and brother. The man Hilly had considered a father growing up. But Hilly and Cam were surrounded by family—Carsons and Delaneys, and the offspring of such calamitous pairings—and Zach was going to walk his baby sister down the aisle.

So he did, bringing her to a man he loved like a brother anyway. And he watched two people pledge their love to each other with the woman he loved seated next to him.

When the wedding ended, and the interminable pictures that tested his leg's endurance were done, they all drove back over to Bent to have the reception at Rightful Claim—filled to the brim with couples. Laurel and Vanessa made rounds with their girls in their arms before handing them off to Grady and Dylan respectively. Noah's adopted son ran around squealing as Addie looked tired with a little baby bump popping more each day. Jen had looked suspiciously nauseated for the past week—at least that was what Lucy had told him that Laurel had told her.

Lucy had jumped into Carson and Delaney life like she'd been born into it, and no one here called her Daisy Delaney, because she was Lucy Cooper here.

Except to Cam, on occasion.

Speaking of which, Grady and Lucy took the small makeshift stage shoved into the corner of the saloon's main room.

"All right, folks, we're going to have the first dance for Cam and Hilly, with our very, *very* special guest to serenade our couple. You all know her as Lucy Cooper, but let's give a warm round of applause for Daisy Delaney."

Everyone clapped, Zach cheered and whistled and Lucy took to the stage with her guitar. She grinned at the crowd and spoke into the microphone.

"When Hilly asked me if I'd sing Cam's favorite song at their wedding, I promised I would. But I also thought something as momentous as a first dance should be about two people, two families, coming together. A song about love and promises. So with Hilly's permission, I wrote a song not just for this moment, but for all of you, too. For love and family and hope. We'll save Cam's favorite song for later, and here's a tip. Get me drunk enough, I'll sing anything. But for now, this one's for all of you."

The crowd laughed, but it didn't take long for them to settle. For Daisy's amazing voice to fill the saloon. What's more, the words of the song Lucy had written, about love and forever and even a few lines about breaking curses, settled over a group made up of people who'd been brave enough to buck tradition and expectation and fall in love with the person they were never even supposed to tolerate.

Silence, tears, happy and hopeful smiles. Even the babies were quiet until Lucy finished her song.

She slid off the stage as Cam and Hilly still swayed to their own music while Grady hooked up the speakers to Hilly's curated playlist for the evening.

Though Lucy stopped and talked to anyone who called out her name, her eyes were on Zach's as she slowly made her way over.

When she finally reached him, she sized him up. "How's the leg, champ?"

"Good enough for a dance."

"So long as it's one and only one," she returned, letting him pull her into his arms. They swayed to the slow song, and Lucy rested her temple on his cheek.

"I wrote the song for Hilly and Cam, for all of them really, but I never would have had the words if I hadn't found you," she murmured into his ear.

He pulled her closer, overwhelmed by his

love for her and the love in the air. "I never believed in curses. I still don't, but you convinced me to believe in meant-to-be."

And from that day forward in Bent, Wyoming, people didn't mention curses anymore. But they did talk about a love strong enough to stand the test of murder, loss, greed, terror and evil.

And a little bit about how some things are just meant to be.

\* \* \* \* \*